We Hunt Monsters
Book One

Aaron Oster

For my wife. Thank you for all the inspiration!

Contents

Prologue

1
2
3
4
5
6
7
8
9
10
11
12
13
14
15
16
17
18
19
20
21
22
23
24
25
26
27

28
29
30
31
32
33
34
35
36
37
38
39
40
41
42
43
44
45
46
47
48
49
50
51
Epilogue
Afterword

Prologue

Keith spun his naginata around in a sweeping blow, the blade glittering red in the moonlight. It easily slid through his opponent's defenses, slicing through the man's neck and sending yet another unfortunate soul to the afterlife.

He slid his armored hand up the shaft of the weapon, slashing to the side and cutting deep into another's neck. He could feel the grinding of bone as the blade sank deep but didn't allow himself even a moment to stand still and feel satisfied. It would be foolish to do when enemies surrounded him on all sides and the emperor's life was on the line.

"To me!" the emperor shouted from his mounted position near the center of the battle. "We won't let Shi'na and his dogs take our homes so easily!"

Keith whirled, throwing the long pole of his weapon up in a block, catching the blade racing for his face. It was almost laughably easy with the decades of experience he had with wielding this weapon. Despite his advanced years, these youngsters didn't stand a chance.

His armored foot came up, slamming into the chest of the unfortunate samurai who'd thought he could attack Keith while his back was turned. There was a low grunt as the man was thrown off his feet, landing hard on the muddy, blood-soaked ground, stunned.

Keith didn't need to finish the man off though, as another of his comrades darted in, his sword slicing down and neatly relieving the man of his head.

"Shan! To me!"

Shan, Keith thought, letting out a mental sigh as he ran to the emperor's side.

He had been given that name upon being transported into this world nearly fifty years ago. He'd always hated it. He looked like the foreigner he was, so why couldn't he have kept his name?

A man tried to get in his way, but Keith bowled straight through him, crushing his skull underfoot and sliding past a falling horse to reach the emperor.

The man was young, having recently come into power after his father – one of Keith's dearest friends – had been killed by assassins sent by Shi'na, the daimyo they were now fighting.

"How are you holding up, my friend?" the emperor asked, removing his helm and revealing a sweat-streaked face lined with blood.

"As well as can be expected," Keith said, ignoring the aches and pains collected on this campaign.

It had been months since he'd been home, and he dearly missed his bed. He was getting far too old for wars like this, and yet, he was so close.

Just another few battles before I can-

"Look out!"

The shout came from behind as a loud whistling sounded. With battle instincts honed over decades, Keith lunged, slamming his shoulder into the horse's ribs. The plates of his armor would definitely hurt the beast, but he'd killed more horses than he could count.

The horse screamed, stumbling back and rearing up. The emperor was tossed off, and the flaming boulder smashed into their ranks.

Keith dropped to his stomach, managing to get hit only by a few stray shards, one of which hit him so hard that it cracked a rib. Screams sounded all around him as the old war veteran pulled himself to his feet, his head ringing and side on fire.

All around him lay crushed and burned bodies, screaming soldiers with missing limbs and the lucky few who'd managed to remain unscathed. Keith looked around blearily, finally spotting the emperor, lying on the ground a few feet away.

He rushed over, seeing that his actions had managed to save the man's life, though he seemed to have broken his leg in the fall. The horse lay a few feet away, its skull having been crushed by a chunk of debris thrown up by the flaming projectile.

"How the mighty have fallen!"

Keith turned, cursing under his breath as a figure dressed in gleaming red armor strode through the center of the carnage.

"Shi'na, you dog," the emperor yelled from the ground. "It's just like you to attack, despite the fact that your own men would be caught in the blast."

"A small price to pay," Shi'na said, his voice sounding pleased from behind his men-yoroi mask, "for a chance to kill a brat who does not know his place."

"You seem quite confident," Keith said, raising his naginata. "What makes you think you can get through to the emperor before reinforcements arrive?"

"Numbers and strategy," Shi'na said, then gestured.

Seven warriors dressed in red armor, signifying his honor guard, charged in from the surroundings, all heading for the emperor.

This better be the last freaking test, Keith thought as he sprang into action. He knew it would take perhaps a minute for the emperor to be found by his forces, so all he had to do was hold out for sixty seconds at a seven-to-one disadvantage. It was hardly a fair fight – for them, that was.

Keith's naginata turned into a glittering whirl of death, parrying two katanas and slicing an arrow out of the air. He stepped over the emperor, stabbing out and catching one of the attackers in the shoulder. Their armor was tougher than the average, so he failed to sever the limb.

Ripping it free, Keith kicked out, catching an enemy fighter in the knee, then swept the heavy steel ball at the other end of his staff into another one's helmet. He felt the satisfying feedback travel through his arm as he killed the man but was forced to step back to parry another blade.

"One old man will not stand between me and the last emperor," Shi'na snarled as his men failed to budge Keith from where he stood.

The daimyo drew his blade and charged, apparently intending to join the battle himself. Keith spun and whirled with the weapon, becoming one with the blade. He cut two more down, then kicked out another's knee, slamming the blade down into his throat.

The others backed off, apparently afraid of him – and who could blame them?

"Shan, avenge my father," the emperor ordered. "Kill that dog!"

"With pleasure," Keith said, then lunged at the man.

Shi'na was an accomplished swordsman – one of the best in the empire, in fact – but he couldn't stand up to Keith, who had decades of experience on the battlefield. Being good in a duel of honor was one thing. Having success on a battlefield was quite another.

Shi'na dove into a series of slashes, his sword glittering as light danced off the blade. Keith took a single step forward and kicked him between his legs with all his strength. The man collapsed to the ground with a high-pitched yelp, and Keith proceeded to jam his blade down the man's throat.

"Shan!" the emperor yelled.

Keith whirled at the sound of the warning, seeing another of Shi'na's guards practically on top of him, blade poised above his head. Keith tugged on his blade, intending to pull up for a block, but it remained stuck in the dead man's face.

Cursing, Keith threw an arm up as the blade came down. Agony flashed through him as the katana cleaved cleanly through his arm and headed straight for his face.

Keith saw death approaching and had only one thing to say. "Poop."

A world of darkness greeted Keith as he opened his eyes. He let out a sigh. He wanted to be angry, to yell and scream. He had been so close to making it free of that world, and he had died thanks to a blade getting stuck in an enemy's corpse.

"I believe that makes eight deaths due to a bladed weapon. You really should stop using those."

Keith let out an internal sigh, then willed himself to rotate. He didn't have a physical form here, but seeing as how he had found himself in this place a total of twelve times now, he was well-versed in how this void behaved.

A man came into view as Keith turned, though 'man' was a bit of a misnomer. Keith actually wasn't sure what this being was, as it had always remained behind its mask. It was colored black and white, evenly split down the middle with a smiling face on the white side and a sad face on the black.

Raven-colored hair rose in spikes above the mask, while the rest of the creature was cloaked in a blue pinstriped suit. Black gloves covered his hands, and shiny black boots covered his feet. Keith assumed they were a man, due to their masculine voice. But he could just as easily be something completely different under there and was simply using a man's voice to throw him off.

"You know, I would almost think you'd planned that to happen," Keith said, his tone accusatory.

"Why, whatever do you mean?" The Trickster asked, affecting a tone that implied surprise.

There was a reason Keith had begun calling this being The Trickster in his mind. The fact that he couldn't be trusted was foremost among them.

"I'm a single battle away from winning and completing our bargain, yet somehow I end up dead."

"I can hardly be blamed for a faulty weapon," The Trickster said with a shrug.

Keith blew out a breath, feeling his annoyance climbing.

"Then why is it that I keep ending up in worlds that use predominantly bladed weapons?" He retorted.

"You could always use a long-range weapon, like a bow or sling," The Trickster offered.

"I've already tried that and still ended up here," Keith said, feeling the fight go out of him.

"You were the one who agreed to the deal," The Trickster said, amusement clear in his voice. "I have your contract right here."

Keith stared at the piece of parchment, the one with his name scrawled on the bottom in uneven lettering. The deal was supposed to be a simple one. Keith would be taken to another world. If he lasted a certain amount of time, he would be returned home, his family would be removed from poverty and have good, happy lives.

At the time, he'd believed he was doing what was best for his two brothers. Their parents had both been killed in an accident several years before, and he'd been struggling to make ends meet. Then this creature had appeared to him with an extremely enticing offer.

What Keith hadn't realized was that the deal would never end. After dying on the first world, he'd thought that was it. However, when he'd reappeared here, he had learned the truth. Until he fulfilled his contract, he would never die. Instead, he would be reborn over and over again, forced to challenge new worlds in hopes of meeting their goal.

How long had it been since he'd made that deal with this creature? Four, maybe five hundred years? His shortest life had been on the second world – a stone-age planet that was scorching at the best of times. He'd only lasted eight years before dying by way of a fist-sized stone to the skull.

This last world was a version of his home planet, Earth, in its Edo period Japan. There had been several differences, he was sure, though Keith hadn't known much about 1600s Japan back when he'd been on Earth, so he wouldn't be able to point them out.

"Why so glum?" The Trickster asked as the parchment rolled back up before it was tucked away inside his suit.

"Because I lived on that world for over fifty years," Keith retorted. "I had friends there. Family. A home. Now I'll never be able to go back."

This was also one of the hardest parts about constantly being reborn. He'd tried maintaining distance at first, just as he did on every world, but time and loneliness had worn him down.

"You already *have* a family," The Trickster said, pulling a picture of his two brothers from his pocket. "Or have you forgotten what you're fighting for?"

"I haven't forgotten," Keith replied, his voice cold. "It's just been so long since I've last seen them."

He paused for a moment, thinking.

"I would like to renegotiate our deal," he finally said.

"Oh?" The Trickster asked. "Do tell."

"I want this next world to be my last," Keith replied.

He'd tried this several times, and it had failed every time he'd brought it up.

"Very well," The Trickster said.

"You're a real piece of-! Wait, what?" Keith asked, coming up short.

"You've provided me with endless entertainment over the last four-hundred-and-twelve years," The Trickster said. "I'm willing to renegotiate our deal, but only under my conditions."

Keith nodded carefully, though he already suspected he would be getting a terrible deal.

"I crank up the difficulty to the maximum in this next world. If you succeed, I will revive your parents and return you to your world at the moment from which I first plucked you. However, if you die, you will remain as my servant forever. But, seeing as I am benevolent, your siblings will still have happy and comfortable lives, regardless of whether you're there or not."

"What's the catch?" Keith asked, thinking that this deal was too good to be true.

"No catch," The Trickster said, removing a contract from his suit and opening it with an exaggerated flourish. "Just sign on the dotted line, and our new pact will be sealed."

Keith snatched the parchment from the creature's hands and read it carefully. He had been tricked once and would not fall for something else. However, after scanning it several times, Keith could see no way to misinterpret the contract.

"I can agree to your terms," Keith said. "But, only on one condition."

"Is that so?" The Trickster asked. "Is my offer not good enough?"

"I want a guide in this new world," Keith said. "If the difficulty will be at the maximum level, I need someone who will help me navigate."

"Done," The Trickster said, adding it to the contract with a flourish.

After examining the document several more times, Keith finally signed it, feeling as though a great weight had suddenly settled on his shoulders.

After centuries, he was getting a chance to not only give his siblings a good life but to revive his dead parents. He was not going to mess this up, regardless of the difficulty. Keith had amassed a vast amount of experience in his previous lives. He just hoped it would be useful in the world in which he was placed.

"Good luck," The Trickster said, bowing at the waist. "You're going to need it."

Before Keith could say anything else, The Trickster vanished, and the world around him went completely black.

1

Welcome to Raiah…

The world of darkness vanished as a message in bright green lettering scrolled across his view. Keith was momentarily confused. This had never happened before. Normally, the Trickster would leave, the area around him would go dark, and then he would find himself in the new world.

Just what sort of world is he sending me to? Keith thought as the message vanished.

However, more words soon appeared, the same green letters scrolling across his vision and giving him more details. At the same time, a feminine voice with a hint of a European accent echoed in his mind, speaking the words as he read them.

This world is governed by the ARK system, a state-of-the-art intelligence that will create contracts, jobs, quests, items, and much more. Pay attention to all messages that ARK provides, as they will determine your experience in this world.

The message disappeared as soon as he finished reading it, and a new one appeared in its place. This time, though, it was only a single word.

Initializing…

Keith watched the small dots flowing across his vision, already knowing that he wasn't going to have an easy time in Raiah.

A videogame world, Keith thought with a groan.

He had never been into videogames – he'd never had the time – but his youngest brother, Jack, had. He'd have to listen to Jack blabbing about this or that, so he was familiar enough with the idea that he knew what it would be like. However, the amount of knowledge he had would give him just enough to *think* he understood.

Keith would've rathered gone to a world where he knew nothing. This way, he wouldn't be thrown off when something unexpected happened. From previous experience, he knew that knowing just a little bit about a subject was a dangerous thing. He just hoped he'd be able to fight his instincts and take everything with a grain of salt.

Color blinded him as the green text vanished, effectively snapping him from his thoughts, the world coming into focus as though through the lens of a camera.

However, unlike a simple lens, the sensation attacked all of his senses at once. Cold air rushed into his lungs as it washed over his skin, sending a chill down his spine. Looking down, he saw a smooth hand, one covered by a rough cotton shirt, stopping just before his elbow.

He extended both arms, stretching this way and that, enjoying the feeling of being in a youthful body once more. Even as he stretched, he examined his surroundings.

The ground underfoot was rocky, with a few sparse blades of grass poking through the rough soil. A slope fell off to one side, turning in a series of jagged peaks and valleys before flattening out some hundred yards below. Turning, Keith looked up, seeing the mountain continuing to rise, where it disappeared from sight as it met the sky, which was a clear blue, with spots of drifting white dotting its surface, and a bright orb shining high. Before and behind, a winding path stretched, disappearing around a bend and showing several more mountains.

Keith stretched backward, taking stock of his situation. He was on the side of a mountain. It was cold, but not cold enough to be winter. By his estimate, it was perhaps a week or two away. It was currently just past noon, which meant he would have about five hours before it was too dark to travel.

The first thing to do would be to find a way off the mountain and make some sort of shelter for the night, he thought. Once he did that, he could search for a source of running water. His mind whirled, thinking of all the next steps that would benefit him.

Keith almost jumped when text flowed across his left eye, and the same female voice spoke directly into his mind. He'd almost forgotten that this was a game world.

You have successfully spawned into your new body. To see your status and hear explanations, simply think the word 'status.'

Keith wasn't going to ignore a message from the system – it had very clearly told him not to – so he did as he was told and thought 'status.' However, almost as soon as he did, a message flashed across his vision, followed by another, and another, and another.

You have learned the skill: Swords…
You have learned the skill: Daggers…
You have learned the skill: Polearms…
You have learned the skill…

Keith stared as the text formed and vanished almost faster than he could read. Finally, after about the fiftieth message, everything disappeared, leaving him with a view of the barren mountainside once more. For several moments, he wondered if the system in this world might be faulty before a new message scrolled across his left eye.

*The skills one has gathered in their previous lives are automatically transferred over with you when entering this world. Seeing as how you've managed to gather **a lot of them**, they have been condensed into single skills.*
Please see your status…

There was a point in the message that appeared in bold lettering, making Keith wonder if he'd somehow aggravated the system. However, his status finally appeared as the message vanished, and he was eager to see what this world would give him at his starting point.

Status
Name: Keith
Race: Human
Class: None
Level: 1
XP: 0/100

HP: 80/80
MP: 0/0
STA: 110/110

Stats

Strength - 10
Vitality - 8
Endurance - 11
Agility - 9
Intelligence - 0
Wisdom - 12
Luck - 5

Skills

Passive
Bladed Mastery: Advanced - IX
Ranged Mastery: Intermediate - IV
Martial Arts: Master - V
Peak Health: Advanced - VIII
Tactician: Advanced - IV
Quick Learner: Advanced - V
Ranger: Advanced - II
Punisher: Master - I
Discerning Eye: Advanced - VIII

Active
None

Equipped Items

Armor
Wool Shirt
Wool Pants
Cloth Shoes

Weapons
None

He carefully read the status over, noting each part of his status. The first section of his status was pretty self-explanatory, though there were a few interesting points to see. The fact that the status listed his race likely meant that there were other sentient races on this world, something he had yet to come across in his many lifetimes.

He was at level one, which was to be expected. He assumed there were ways to gain experience, or XP as the status called it, by doing quests and completing other such tasks. The only thing he wanted was an explanation on was the 'class' tab. He concentrated on it, and new text replaced his status to answer his question.

Class: A class can only be bestowed in one of two ways, either by a class trainer or from a class book. Choosing a class is extremely important, as it will determine the path you take in Raiah. More on classes will be explained when a class trainer or book is found.

The message vanished when he finished reading, leaving Keith to examine the next part of his status. Here, he wanted a better understanding of what his stats did, so he pulled up the explanation.

HP: Your total health points are very important. If your HP goes to zero, you die. Health regeneration depends on level.

Pretty simple but to the point, Keith thought, moving on to the next.

MP: Your total mana points determine how much magic you can use. It's completely useless unless you get a class that uses magic.

Keith minded having zero MP a lot less now. He wasn't really the magic type anyway. His experience always lay in physical combat, and although he hadn't been in a world that relied on this form of magic before, he *had* been in worlds that used other types. In one world, the citizens had grown their power through the martial arts, while another channeled power through runes.

He had stuck with the physical route through it all and was planning on staying that way.

STA: Your total stamina determines how long you can keep going. Run out of this, and you'll fall flat on your face. Stamina regeneration depends on level.

Okay, Keith thought. *Much more important to make sure this stays high.*

If he ran out of stamina in the middle of a fight, it would mean his end.

Stats: There are seven total stats that determine your overall strength. Each number gives you a quantified value, showing how proficient you are in each. Each level will give you five stat points to allocate. Make these choices carefully, as they will determine your future growth.

Strength: Determines physical strength. If you're not strong, you can't lift heavy things.

Vitality: This determines your total HP. Every point gives you ten health.

Endurance: This determines your total STA. Every point gives you ten to your stamina.

Agility: Determines quickness and dexterity. If you're not fast, things can hit you more easily.

*Intelligence: This doesn't determine **actual** intelligence. It just determines total MP. Every point gives you ten MP. This stat will only be unlocked upon receiving an appropriate Class.*

*Wisdom: This doesn't determine **actual** wisdom. It just determines how fast and how capably you learn.*

Luck: Pretty self-explanatory...

Keith wasn't sure what a good stat was, but from what he could see, there were a few things that would be important for him to raise. Strength was at the top, followed closely by agility. He was assuming his health could be bolstered if he wore armor, but that would need to come later.

He was about to read a bit further down the list when another message superimposed itself above his status.

*Quest: **A World to Conquer** has been accepted.*

*Quest Available: **Civilization***
It's quite cold on the side of this mountain, isn't it? You'll probably want to reach somewhere warm before dark.
Difficulty: C
Rewards: 50 XP, 5 bronze coins
Time Remaining: 5 hours

This quest had been automatically accepted

Okay... Keith thought as the message vanished, along with his status.

It seemed that he didn't have a choice but to take this quest. He decided he could check out the rest of his status later, as the quest had a timer, and he didn't want to fail the first one. So, he began to walk, heading east down the mountain path.

2

As he walked, Keith noticed two small bars appear in the corner of his vision – a green and a yellow one. The yellow seemed to be twitching, emptying a tiny drop before immediately refilling. He took this to mean that he was in good enough shape that his stamina would basically remain at the maximum so long as he stayed at a walk.

He decided to speed up a bit to test how fast he could run before his stamina really began to run out. At a light jog, it began slowly ticking down, the process speeding up as he did. When at a flat run, Keith estimated he could maintain for about half a minute before he completely ran out.

That's odd, he thought as he slowed to a walk. He knew he should be able to run faster than this – he had in the previous world, even as an old man. It took him a couple of minutes to figure it out, and when he did, he felt like smacking himself.

His agility wasn't high enough to support his full speed. He would need to do more tests to see what his limits were in his new body, as well as note the changes as he grew in level. He paid attention to how quickly his stamina regenerated as he slowed to a normal walk.

About one per second.

If he completely emptied his stamina, it would currently take 110 seconds to fully restore, thanks to his endurance of eleven.

As he went on, the trail began to thin, being overtaken by bigger stones that soon turned to boulders. However, he found that he had no trouble picking out the correct path, his mind somehow always pointing it out as he went. He was a bit puzzled by this, until he remembered the list of skills he'd been given upon entering this world.

He wondered if there was a way to view skills while walking, and as though answering his unspoken question, his skills appeared once more. Only this time, they were translucent so he could read and view the path ahead at the same time.

Skills: Skills are divided into two categories, passive and active.

Passive skills: Skills that are always in effect and do not require any additional cost.

Active skills: Skills that require a cost of stamina or mana to activate.

Passive skills can be learned by performing certain actions, from Skill Books, or through a trainer. Active skills can only be learned through Skill Books or through a trainer. They cannot be learned by oneself.

Skills are automatically relearned upon entering the world, matching your previous level of skill. This is why skills were awarded upon entry to the world.

*Skills level up as you use them, and more advanced versions of the skill become available as you move through the ranks. In order, these ranks are **Novice, Beginner, Intermediate, Advanced, Master, Grandmaster,** and **Sage**. Only those at the level of **Master** and above can teach their skills to others.*

Each rank contains ten levels, after which you advance to the next rank in the skill. The higher-ranked a skill is, the better it will be.

This explanation was a bit more thorough than the last, but Keith was happy, as he thought he understood. What he was really curious about was how his learned skills stacked up to others who were already living in this world. He'd scanned through the skills earlier, and now understood that he had several high-level skills already, likely due to the hundreds of years of experience he'd racked up over his dozen lifetimes.

Since he could travel and read at the same time, Keith decided to pull up his skills and see their descriptions.

Bladed Mastery
Level: Advanced - IX
All bladed weapons up to legendary rarity can be wielded regardless of restriction or condition.

+175% Damage, +150% Accuracy, +100% Armor piecing, +350% Critical

Keith felt a pang in his chest as he read over the first skill's description. He might not have known a lot about games, but he knew enough about basic math to know that this skill would give him an overwhelming advantage with bladed weapons. It was a shame that he would absolutely refuse to use one in this world.

Eight of his last twelve deaths were caused by a bladed weapon. He wasn't about to tempt fate for a ninth time. He pulled up the next skill, knowing that it would be good and already regretting his decision to forgo weapons.

Ranged Mastery
Level: Intermediate - IV
All ranged weapons up to epic rarity can be wielded, regardless of restriction or condition.
+145% Damage, +125% Accuracy, +80% Armor piercing, +290% Critical

Keith went straight to the next skill, excited about this one.

Martial Arts
Level: Master - V
You are a master of unarmed combat. You don't need weapons to fight. As a Master in this skill, active skills may become available to you.
+200% Damage, +170% Accuracy, +110% Armor piercing, +415% Critical
*You may teach this skill to others

Keith grinned.
Now that's more like it!
Finally, a skill that would come in handy, and thankfully, it was the one he actually cared about. Fighting unarmed would assure he could never be killed by getting a blade stuck or missing a shot with a bow or sling. Sure, it carried greater risk, but so long as he was careful, he should be able to thrive.

He went through his other skills, feeling excited that he seemed to have such a large advantage right at the start.

Peak Health
Level: Advanced - VIII
You are at peak physical health. Mana, stamina and health will regenerate at a faster pace. You will recover from wounds faster and will take less damage while in battle.
+50% Increased HP, MP & STA regen, +100% Recovery speed, -35% Damage

Tactician
Level: Advanced - IV
You have a discerning mind toward combat, as well as in everyday life. You can spot deception, plan a battle, and cannot be tricked by anyone below your own skill level.

Quick Learner
Level: Advanced - V
You have a keen mind for learning and understanding the way of the world.
+75% Chance to learn new skills, +50% Growth to all skills

Ranger
Level: Advanced - II
You have ranged far and wide. You can track, hunt, forest, climb, and swing. Any rough terrain is no match for you.
+200% Chance to find hidden trails, +50% Movement speed in rough terrain

Punisher
Level: Master - I
You were never one to allow your enemies to escape. You punish all with brutal efficiency. All of your blows strike twice as hard. As a Master in this skill, active skills may become available to you.
+100% Critical, +100% Damage if struck first
*You may teach this skill to others

Discerning Eye
Level: Advanced - VIII
You can analyze your surroundings, identifying anything below level 75 at a glance. You can spot hidden treasures that others might miss, and you can identify the value of items.

Keith let out a breath, thinking over everything he had just read. He didn't know this for certain, but it seemed that his centuries of experience had put him far ahead of the curve. Of course, he was still at level one, so something more powerful could probably squash him, but so long as he was careful and gained enough levels, he should be strong enough to beat this world's objective.

Speaking of...

Keith pulled up his open quests. He did this in the same way he'd pull up his status. Before he looked at his quests though, he read through the explanation.

Quests: Quests are generated in many ways, but in simple terms, a quest is a contract. Complete the objectives set out, and you will be rewarded.

*Quests range in difficulty, and the more difficult the quest, the higher the reward. In order, the difficulty levels are **C, B, A, S, SS, SSS** and **World**.*

That was simple enough. Keith navigated down to his open quests and read the first one that had been automatically accepted.

A World to Conquer
*Being a conqueror isn't easy. Too bad you have no choice. There are five continents on Raiah. You must challenge and defeat the **World Monster** on each continent.*
Difficulty: World
Current Objective: Defeat Orne Skull-stomper, Elder Troll of Humania
Current Reward: 100,000 XP, 1 world item, 5 legendary monster pieces, 3 large gold bars
Progress: 0/5 Defeated

Keith gaped, not only at the sheer difficulty of the quest but at the reward for completing a fifth of it. And to think that he had to complete the entire quest in order to fulfill his contract.

The Trickster wasn't kidding when he said he'd be turning up the difficulty, Keith thought sourly.

Still, he would make the best of what he had, and seeing as two more unknowns popped up as he'd been reading, he decided to pull them up.

Currency: The currency in Raiah is simple. Bronze coins, silver coins, small gold bars and large gold bars. 100 bronze coins go into a silver, 100 silver into a small gold, 10 small gold into a large.

Items: Items can fall into several categories, including weapons, armor, crafting materials, and ores.

*In order of rarity, these are: **Common, uncommon, rare, epic, legendary,** and **world.***

Once more, no further information was available, and this time, Keith wished there *was*. He wanted to know more about items, seeing as he definitely needed some armor. Well, sturdier than what he was currently wearing.

He was about to pull up his 'items' tab when his eyes locked onto a set of peculiar prints in the ground. They shone a bright purple, despite the sunlight beaming down from above, and judging by the imprints near the toes, this would be some sort of predator.

Lifting his eyes, Keith could see the tracks heading deeper into the mountain, and seeing as that was where he was currently headed, he had a bad feeling that he would be running into trouble soon.

3

"How did I know I'd be right?" Keith muttered to himself as he pressed his back flat against the boulder.

He was currently trying his very best not to be noticed by the mouth of fur and claws just a few feet away. He'd really been hoping that he could avoid running into this monster. He had debated turning back, but he'd already traveled over two hours in this direction, and with no other way down the mountain, he would most assuredly fail his first quest.

Keith peered around the side of the boulder, looking down the small slope between him and the hairy creature. He wasn't quite sure what it was, as he had never seen anything like it. It stood on four thick and muscular legs, and its body was covered in shaggy brown fur. It must have been around five feet at the shoulder, with a pair of small black eyes and snout poking from a squished-looking face.

However, the long black talons and gleaming teeth as the creature snuffled gave him more than enough reason to stay away. Thankfully, this creature seemed to be busy with something stuck up in one of the few trees near the bottom of the hill, meaning that Keith had a pretty good chance of sneaking by.

The monster let out a snuffling roar, then rose up on two legs and clawed at the bark. Keith took a deep breath, then leaped from cover, dashing behind another boulder.

"Hey, watch it!"

Keith froze upon hearing that voice. It was loud, shrill, and filled with terror. He quickly peered around the boulder, wondering if a person had gotten trapped up there. A small creature with colorful fur and a ringed tail leaped from one of the branches, waving small arms and staring right at him.

"Help! Yes, you, the guy peeking out from behind that boulder. Help me! I don't wanna die."

Keith slid behind the boulder again, shaking his head and wondering if he'd lost his mind. That monkey was very obviously talking to him, but monkeys weren't supposed to talk, right?

A small *ping* sounded in his mind, and a moment later, a message scrolled across his vision.

*Quest available: **Save the day***
A monkey has been trapped in a tree. Why don't you go rescue it?
Difficulty: C
Rewards: 300 XP, World guide

...This quest had been automatically accepted

"Oh, that low-down, devious piece of...," Keith growled as he realized that The Trickster had managed to screw him over yet again.

The creature had agreed to give him a world guide, but he had never specified where the guide would be. Leave it to that thing to make him have to fight for his life to get it.

"That guide *better* be worth it," Keith muttered as he cast about for something to use.

He currently knew nothing about this creature, so he didn't want to risk charging in blindly, especially with those claws and teeth. Not to mention the fact that the monster had to outweigh him by at least a factor of four.

His gaze finally landed on a small rock with jagged edges. He stooped, lifting it and bouncing it in his palm. Turning, he peered around the boulder once more, wondering what level this creature was. Although he didn't know much about games, he was smart enough to put two and two together.

A higher level meant a stronger opponent.

As though answering his question, the creature was suddenly outlined in purple, and text appeared floating over its head.

Snout-Nosed Ripper
Level: 2
HP: 140/140

Several spots of darker purple appeared at the same time, behind its skull, at its throat, in the joints of the knees, and a spot on its shoulders.

For a moment, Keith was confused, up until he remembered his Tactician and Discerning Eye skills. With those two helping him, this battle should – in theory – be far easier to complete. Despite this monster being level two, this quest *was* still rated with a C difficulty, which meant that the system believed he could easily beat it.

The ripper let out a roar, then reared up on its hind legs and raked the tree with its claws, eliciting another scream from the monkey.

"You don't want to eat me," the monkey yelled. "I'm all fur and bones!"

Letting out a breath, Keith spun out from behind the boulder, then threw the stone, aiming for one of the patches of darker purple on the ripper's hide.

The stone whizzed through the air and struck the exact spot he'd been aiming for – the back of its exposed left knee. It seemed his Ranged Mastery skill actually did help, even if it was something as simple as a thrown rock.

The ripper let out a small yelp, and a message popped up in the corner of Keith's vision.

-12, Critical

The ripper's HP bar dipped a bit, removing any doubt about what that message had just told him. It seemed his hunch had been correct. The darker spots on the monster's body were weak points, and seeing as he had bonuses when striking critical areas, he'd been able to do a fair amount of damage.

However, throwing the rock had the unfortunate side effect of getting the monster's attention.

The ripper shoved itself off the tree, whirling to face the now-exposed Keith. The small, beady red eyes bore into his own, and a pair of gleaming fangs, dripping with saliva, poked from its bottom lip.

The monster opened its mouth and let out a roar, then charged right at him. Keith, having faced down many an opponent on the battlefield, did what any sensible man would do.

He turned and ran.

His stamina began falling as soon as he did, and Keith paid careful attention to it. He knew the monster would be faster than him, so there was really no point in running, but with as much health as it had, he needed to whittle it down before fighting it head-on.

The ripper came skidding around the boulder, its talon-like claws skittering over the loose stones underfoot, and Keith winged another stone at its face. This one struck it straight in the eye, causing the monster to stumble back.

-15, Critical

Snout-Nosed Ripper is blinded in one eye.

Now that's interesting, Keith thought as the monster shook its head. Dark blood streamed from the eye he'd struck, giving him a huge advantage. So, he did what any sensible person would do in this situation. He charged right at the monster, stooping to scoop up another stone as he did. He wanted to approach from its blind side, but a boulder was in his way.

The ripper, seeing him coming, reared up, its hooked talons swiping at his chest. Keith hurled the stone, nailing the monster's exposed sensitive area.

-30, Massive Critical

Snout-Nosed Ripper is stunned for 5 seconds.

*Snout-Nosed Ripper will never have children again. I think we all know who the **real** monster here is.*

The ripper let out a horrific squeal, then toppled backward, its body frozen in place. Keith, still running, reached the monster just as it fell and leaped in the air, bringing his leg down in a powerful ax-kick right on its skull.

In his many lifetimes, he'd practiced all forms of martial arts – it was likely why his Martial Arts skill was as high as it was – and the result was quite spectacular. The kick landed with all the force and momentum of his run. A loud *crack* echoed over the mountainside as blood sprayed from the point of impact.

-40, Massive Critical

Keith pulled his leg back, and in a single, smooth motion, he dropped to one knee, driving his fist into the same spot. Warm blood coated his fist as he drove it part-way into the monster's skull, earning him another whimper of pain from the creature.

-38, Massive Critical

With this last attack, Keith saw the monster's health plummet to the point where there was just a tiny sliver of red remaining in the HP bar floating above its head. He quickly pulled his arm up to finish the monster and made the mistake of trying to end the battle without first checking on the condition of his enemy.

With a roar, the ripper leaped to its feet, its talon-like claws slashing out and tearing a long series of bloody gashes across Keith's chest. His vision flashed red for a moment, then a message flashed in the corner of his left eye.

-42 damage, you are bleeding

-5 HP per second for the next 5 seconds.

The most shocking part about that strike wasn't the burning pain in his chest, nor the blood gushing down his torso, nor was it the fact that his HP started quickly ticking down. No, the most shocking part about that attack was that the system hadn't identified it as a 'critical' one.

This meant that even with his skills – skills that reduced all taken damage – this monster had shaved away over half his health with a single attack.

The ripper lunged with its mouth open wide, and Keith twisted to one side, just barely managing to avoid taking an attack head-on.

-2 damage

Keith's eyes flicked to his own health bar, which was now dangerously low, even as it ticked down again, thanks to his bleeding status. He was too off-balance to strike back. Thankfully, the ripper needed to recover after missing its attack, turning its head to appraise him with its still-working eye.

Keith took a step back as the monster turned, snout bunched up and growling. While it had taken several critical attacks to bring the monster to this point, a single attack had nearly done him in.

His health ticked down once more, and the bleeding finally stopped. In total, he had lost a whopping 67 HP from that one attack, and including the grazing attack the ripper had managed to land, he had 11 health left.

I am not *going to die just a couple of hours after coming to this world!* Keith thought, squaring his shoulders and preparing for the monster's next attack.

The ripper lunged, but the instant before it did, Keith saw its muscles tense, giving away the coming attack. Even as the ripper threw itself forward, claws raking out to end him, Keith dove as well, tucking into a roll and coming up under the monster.

He was in too close to punch as the monster came down, so he tucked his arm in and drove his elbow up and into the creature's ribs. A jarring sensation ran up through his shoulder, and a small *-4* flashed before him.

Oh, no! Keith thought as he was driven to the ground, the monster having lived on a single point of health.

The wind was knocked from his lungs, while another damage notification flashed in his vision.

-6 damage

The monster writhed around on top of him, trying to get off so that it could attack him again. From his prone position on his back, Keith didn't exactly have a great angle and knew he wouldn't be dealing much damage.

His hand scrabbled around for a few frantic moments as the monster backed off. A pair of gleaming eyes appeared, just inches from his own, and he felt his short hair being ruffled by a blast of steaming breath so foul it made his eyes water.

The ripper opened its mouth wide and roared in his face. Keith took the opening and proceeded to jam the rock he'd found right down its throat.

-9, Critical

Snout-Nosed Ripper dies.

+75 XP

The monster let out a gurgling sound, then collapsed sideways, its single good eye rolling up in its bloodied skull and its body going limp. Keith simply laid there, his chest heaving as he tried to calm down from his latest near-death experience.

4

*Congratulations! You have completed the quest: **Save the Day**.*

+300 XP

Level Up!
Congratulations! You have reached level 2. You have 5 Stat Points to allocate.

Level Up!
Congratulations! You have reached level 3. You have 5 Stat Points to allocate.

Keith blinked past the numerous messages that assaulted him and found a small creature sitting on his chest. It was the monkey that had been crying for help; that much was obvious, though this had to be the strangest looking monkey Keith had ever seen.

Small black rings surrounded its eyes, making the yellow irises stand out even more than they already did. It was around a foot tall, with rounded ears, a small mouth, and fur flecked blue, gold, and black, as though someone had splattered paint all over its otherwise white fur. Its tail was ringed black and white, like a lemur's, which was the only part about it that looked normal.

"Heya," the monkey said, extending a paw. "Thanks for saving my life, pal. Name's Bob, but you can call me Robert. Wait, no, I meant that the other way around."

"Uh, sure," Keith said, extending a hand. "Name's Keith."

Bob grasped his finger and shook it a couple of times, seeming pleased.

"Well, seeing as you're the only sentient being in the immediate area, I take it that you're the one I'm supposed to guide. As far as first impressions go, I'd say you did a heck of a job there, pal."

Bob nodded a few times, as though confirming what he'd just said, before leaping off his chest and landing on a nearby boulder.

"So, you gonna get up? Or are you just going to keep laying there?"

Truthfully, Keith just wanted to stay where he was. His wounds still ached, and although his HP was slowly ticking up, it was still quite low.

"Why was that monster chasing you?" Keith asked, deciding to stay on the ground for the time being.

"Why do monsters do anything?" Bob asked, rolling his eyes. "It was hungry."

The monkey then looked up to the sky and shook his little fist.

"If someone had done their job right and spawned me in the correct spot, this wouldn't have happened!"

"Spawned?" Keith asked, unfamiliar with the term.

"The system creates things all the time," Bob said with a shrug. "I was created for the sole purpose of guiding you through this world. Spawning is the term used to describe the creation of any creature on Raiah."

"Are outsiders common in this world?" Keith asked.

From what the messages had been implying, that seemed to be the case.

"Oh, yeah," Bob replied. "People are showing up here all the time. It's so common, in fact, that nearly a quarter of the residents here once lived on a different world."

"The system says you're a guide," Keith said. "What exactly can you do?"

"I can do a lot," Bob said, puffing out his chest. "I can answer any question about the world, and in far greater detail than the boring system. I can recommend certain quests or items and even tell you where they might be located. I can give you information on which classes would be best based on your skills, as well as how to grow. In other words, I'm awesome."

"But you can't fight," Keith said, pushing himself into a sitting position.

"I am what you might call a 'non-combat entity,'" Bob said, making quotes in the air. "In other words, while I can help you, I myself am helpless when it comes to fighting. Would you give me permission to view your status?"

The sudden change in topic might have been a bit jarring to a normal person, but having dealt with all types of strange people over his many lifetimes, Keith was barely fazed.

"You need permission?" Keith asked.

"I wouldn't be asking if I didn't," Bob replied.

"Okay then," Keith said. "I give you permission to view my status."

If Bob was going to guide him through this world, it could only be to his benefit if the odd creature could see what he was working with.

Speaking of which.

Keith concentrated on the monkey and tried to see his information, just as he had with the monster he'd battled.

Bob (Robert): World Guide
Level: 3
HP: 68/80

"Is your level and health the same as mine?" Keith asked, noting the similarity straight away.

"Uh-huh," Bob said, sounding distracted. "If you die, I die. So, try not to. I've only been alive for a few hours, and I quite like it. Holy cannoli! What the hell kind of monster are you?"

Keith stared at the monkey, feeling a bit worried.

"Is something wrong?" he asked.

"Is something *wrong*?" the monkey asked, looking to him with wide eyes. "I've never seen someone at your level with such high skills."

"To be fair," Keith said. "I'm technically the only person you've ever met."

"You know what I mean," Bob said, waving him off – the monkey seemed quite pleased. "I was afraid I'd get a complete weakling noob! However, it seems that ARK has had mercy after all. Sure, you almost died in your first fight, but that was because you had no armor or active skills. Speaking of, you should have some active skills available to you after that fight. You should check."

"Okay," Keith said, not having understood even half of what the monkey had just said. "How do I do that?"

"Here," Bob said. "Since you gave me permissions, I can pull it up for you."

As soon as the monkey finished talking, a new series of messages appeared before him, this time, contained in a neat, white box.

*New active skills available: **Stonestance, Brutal Rain***

Stonestance
Your body becomes as tough as stone
Cost: 20 STA
Damage: 6-10
Armor: +15%
Duration: 10 Seconds

Brutal Rain
Inflict a punishing series of blows
Cost: 40 STA
Damage: 12-16

After reading the two over, Keith looked to his guide.

"I can understand how the first would be a skill, but how would the second differ from a normal series of attacks? Also, it seems to me that my ordinary attacks would do more damage without me having to pay to use them."

"Firstly," Bob said. "The second attack, Brutal Rain, likely has an effect that we can't yet see. The system does not offer active skills that can be performed without the aid of said skill. Secondly, what you see is only the base damage of the skill. That means that whatever bonuses your passive skills give you will be added on to these.

"Additionally, while that last monster might have been easy to beat, I can assure you that there are monsters that are far tougher. Trust me when I say that you'll be grateful to have them."

"How can I learn these skills then?" Keith asked, thinking that the added damage couldn't hurt.

A new message popped up before his eyes.

*You have learned the active skills: **Stonestance** and **Brutal Rain***

"Well, that was easier than I expected," Keith said, blinking away the message. "How do I use them?"

The passive skills were easy enough, as they worked in the background, but these active ones would obviously require some sort of trigger, or they would sap his stamina away until he had nothing left.

"Easy," Bob said, hopping onto his shoulder as Keith stood, his wounds having completely healed – which he considered to be quite miraculous. "Just think about activating the skill, and the system will do the rest. Now, I would be happy to answer more questions, but I can see that you've got an active quest with less than two hours left to complete. So, I recommend we get a move-on."

"Probably a good idea," Keith said.

It was starting to get noticeably colder as the time passed, and with his only shirt now in tatters, he didn't think things would be getting much better.

"Can you tell me where the nearest town is?" he asked.

"Of course I can!" Bob said, puffing his chest out. "Follow my lead, and we'll be there with time to spare!"

Keith had barely started walking when the monkey yelled for him to wait.

"What is it?" Keith asked, instantly alert, afraid that another monster might be nearby.

"You forgot to loot the corpse!" Bob exclaimed.

"What?" he asked, now very confused.

"The monster corpse," Bob said. "Go back. It'll have valuable materials that can be used for all kinds of things!"

Keith had done far more disgusting things than skinning an animal in his many lifetimes, so he took the monkey's advice and went over to loot the ripper's corpse. It smelled far worse than Keith remembered, and his nose wrinkled in response.

He crouched, casting about for a sharp rock so that he might skin the creature, when Bob interrupted.

"You don't need to physically skin it," the monkey said, making a disgusted face. "Just place your hand on the monster and think the word 'loot.'"

Keith did as instructed and was greeted by a new me

Snout-Nosed Ripper has been successfully looted.

You have received: 3 Ripper claws, 3 Ripper ribs, Ripper pelt & Ripper spine

The monster shimmered for a moment, then vanished, leaving a small pool of blood in its wake.

"What just happened?" Keith asked. "Also, the system says I got a bunch of items, but I don't see any of them."

"The monster was looted, so it disappeared. The system can't just have random monster corpses everywhere. The world would get cluttered. As for the items, they were all automatically sent to your inventory. Just think the word 'inventory' to access them. Best do it while we're walking, though. We've already wasted enough time."

Keith let out a sigh, then rose to his feet. Bob might be helpful, but he would soon need to put him in his place. After all, he couldn't spend the next who knew how long being ordered around by a monkey.

5

The wind picked up as Keith headed deeper into the mountains, his tattered shirt doing little to keep the cold at bay. Bob had seemingly decided that he was a suitable mode of transportation as he settled onto Keith's shoulder, curling his fluffy tail around his neck. Keith now moved at a quick jog, filtering through the monkey's incessant chattering, picking out what was useful and ignoring the rest.

"You know, if you want to move faster or add to your stamina, you should probably allocate those stat points you got when you leveled up," Bob suggested after they'd been traveling for nearly half an hour.

Keith felt like smacking himself for not realizing this sooner. However, he consoled himself with the knowledge that he'd been distracted by the monkey, as well as what had been going on in the world around him.

He pulled up his status and looked over his stats, taking note of the ones he wanted most to increase. His strength could always use a boost, as could his agility, but both endurance and vitality were important as well.

"How do people decide where to put their stat points if they only get five per level?" Keith asked.

"Most people would only focus on adding to two or three stats at the most," Bob said. "Trying to spread yourself too thin will lead to a build that is ultimately average in everything. However, it's also important to note that you can boost your stats with items. Additionally, a class automatically awards stat points to specific stats with every level you gain."

"So, if I wanted to be a hand-to-hand fighter who wears light to medium armor," Keith said, "where would I put my points now?"

"Firstly, I have to say that fighting monsters bare-handed is probably not a good idea," Bob said. "While you do have a high Martial Arts skill, bare-handed fighting is normally best against those of similar size or stature. Why don't you pick up a sword? You have a pretty good skill level in bladed weapons, and I'm sure that with just a little training, you can bring the skill up to master level."

"Out of the question," Keith said, immediately dismissing the monkey's idea. "I refuse to use bladed weapons, and that's final."

"You're a stubborn one, aren't you?" Bob said, sticking his face right in one of Keith's eyes and obscuring his vision. "Alright then. How about a bow or something similar? You seemed to do pretty well with those rocks earlier."

"I will fight bare-handed," Keith reiterated.

"Any reason you have this strange fixation on beating things to death with your bare hands?" Bob asked.

"No one can disarm me unless they literally *disarm* me," Keith replied. "Weapons have cost me in the past, and I refuse to repeat that mistake."

"Fine," Bob said with a sigh. "Be stubborn about it. If you're going down this route, I'd recommend putting points into strength, agility, and endurance, focusing more on the first two. We'll have to find you some vitality-boosting items and get you some armor though. Remember, if you die, *I* die, and I don't wanna die."

"I'm glad to see you've got your priorities straight," Keith said sarcastically as he went back to his status to assign the points.

He put four into strength, four to agility, and two to endurance. A message popped up asking if he was satisfied with his selection, and he mentally said *yes*. As soon as he did, the point totals updated, and Keith felt a noticeable difference as his speed immediately increased.

His stamina bar updated as he watched, moving from 110 to 130. Actually feeling excited, Keith looked over his status to see the changes made since he'd first entered this world.

Status
Name: Keith
Race: Human
Class: None
Level: 3
XP: 75/300

HP: 80/80
MP: 0/0
STA: 130/130

Strength - 14 (10+4)
Vitality - 8
Endurance - 13 (11+2)
Agility - 13 (9+4)
Intelligence - 0
Wisdom - 12
Luck - 5

Skills

Passive
Bladed Mastery: Advanced – IX
Ranged Mastery: Intermediate – IV
Martial Arts: Master – V
Peak Health: Advanced – VIII
Tactician: Advanced – IV
Quick Learner: Advanced – V
Ranger: Advanced – II
Punisher: Master – I
Discerning Eye: Advanced – VIII

Active
Stonestance: Novice - I
Brutal Rain: Novice - I

Equipped Items

Armor
Wool Shirt
Wool Pants
Cloth Shoes

Weapons
None

It looked like he'd need another 225 XP to get to his next level, which meant that every level required that level's number of experience, times one-hundred. When he voiced his theory aloud, Bob shook his head.

"It's kinda true, but not completely," the monkey said. "The level curve gets significantly steeper every time you grow ten levels. For example, the cost from level nine to ten is nine hundred XP, but the cost from ten to eleven will be more than double."

"So much for this being easy," Keith sighed. "Is there a maximum level one can reach?"

Bob nodded.

"Level one hundred is the maximum, though you're not likely to meet anyone even close to that strong on this continent."

"And what continent are we on?" Keith asked.

"We're on Humania, the human continent," Bob replied. "This is the easiest of the five. In order of difficulty, the other four are Beastland, the Fourliance, the Frigid Seas, and Monstros. You'll probably want to make sure you're at least at level twenty-five before traveling to the next continent, though. Anything weaker, and you'll be dead within the day."

"Did you see my quest to defeat the five World Monsters?" Keith asked, now suspecting that there would be a single one on every continent.

"I did," Bob replied, though he seemed a bit nervous. "World Monsters are basically the toughest creatures on any continent. They are unique monsters, and each has a name. You do *not* want to take one of those on alone.

"A basic monster, like the one we just fought? Sure, fight away. Even a Field Boss of the same level, but anything of Boss-rank or higher will require a team, and World Monsters are as tough as they come."

"With those rewards, I can only imagine," Keith said. "How strong is a world item?"

"World items are exactly as they sound," Bob replied. "They are items with the power to alter the world itself. There is only a single World Item that is well-known on this continent, and that would be in the hands of the Royal Guild, headed by the royal family itself.

"The item is called Barren Wasteland and has the power to basically turn any battlefield into just that. The scariest part about this world item is that it can be used three times, where most world items can only be used once."

A map suddenly appeared, superimposed over Keith's vision.

"Woah! Where did *that* come from? Did I have access to that the whole time?"

"No," Bob replied, already zooming in on an area of the map. "You only got this map because of me."

The map continued zooming in until Keith saw a small red dot, one heading through an area called the Craggy Pass. A small, dotted line followed him, and as Bob zoomed out a bit, he could see a small flag placed on a spot on the map called Oster's Keep.

"This is where you're headed," Bob said as the dotted line was highlighted further. "I won't need to pull this map up unless you specifically want to see it – and I don't see why you would want to when I could just read it for you – but I pulled it up so you could see the effects of a world level item."

The map zoomed out until Keith could see over a dozen small towns and cities. It kept zooming out until the first city – Umber City – came into view. The map continued panning out until he could see the entire continent of Humania. Keith's brow furrowed as he noticed something odd.

"Almost a quarter of this continent is a desert. Is that...Wait, are you saying...?"

"That the Royal Desert was created by Barren Wasteland?" Bob said. "That is, in fact, what I am saying. Before the Royal Guild took over the continent some fifty years ago, this continent was ruled by the Noble Guild, comprised of five dukes and several counts and barons. All King Narbius needed to do was use Barren Wasteland once, and he became the new ruler of the continent."

"An item that could do that can be used two more times?" Keith asked, completely shocked that there was a power so great in this world.

"Yup," Bob replied, closing the map. "Of course, that makes it one of the weaker world items, as most can only be used once."

Keith had a hard time wrapping his mind around something like that. An item that turned a quarter of this continent into a desert was considered one of the weaker ones. If that was the case, then what could a strong one do? Wipe out an entire continent?

He was about to ask when a shadow suddenly blotted out the sun, causing him to peer up. He was initially afraid that a storm might be coming in, but he froze, feeling his heart all but seize up as a massive, winged creature appeared over the top of the mountain pass.

6

"What in the hell is that?" Keith hissed, ducking behind a boulder and feeling his heart begin to race a mile a minute.

He had faced down death thousands of times in his many lifetimes but never had he encountered a creature that exuded such sheer terror.

"You have the Discerning Eye skill," Bob said with a shrug. "I could tell you, of course, but I think using it on that creature will probably do you some good. Plus, it'll help your skill-level go up too."

The monkey seemed oddly calm, despite the literal wall of death flying above, and that calmness rubbed off on Keith.

"I saw the ripper's information before, though I'm not exactly sure how I did it," Keith said.

"Just concentrate on the item in question, and think the word 'analyze,' Bob said. "Make it quick, too. We've got under an hour until your quest timer runs out."

Keith concentrated on the massive shadow above and did as Bob instructed. A purple outline surrounded the creature, and its information appeared, just like last time.

Meir, Deathless Dreadbird (Legendary Monster)
Level: 50
HP: 250,000/250,000

"Woah," Keith whispered, watching Meir with wide eyes as the monster continued to wing its way across the sky. "What's a Legendary Monster?"

"Just as there are World Monsters, there are also Legendary Monsters," Bob said. "The difference is that there are more of them and that they tend to travel. You'll need to be a hell of a lot stronger if you want to take a creature like that on, though. Now, come on, you're running short on time."

The Dreadbird vanished over the mountain pass, disappearing from view. Only once it was gone did Keith start moving again, this time alternating between running and jogging to make up for lost time.

The mountain pass began to grow narrower, turning into a steeper, uphill climb and forcing him to move on all fours at several points. To his surprise, his speed didn't diminish in the slightest.

"It's because of your Ranger skill," Bob said, shading his eyes and peering toward the top of the hill. "You have a bonus to movement speed in rough terrain."

It was also because Keith was moving the way he was that he noticed the deep grooves in the stone. As soon as he did, they were highlighted in purple, moving up the side of the mountain pass that he was currently in.

"Oof, bad luck," Bob groaned as Keith pointed out the tracks. "Maybe it's gone?" the monkey hedged.

A distant roar echoed through the mountain pass as though to counteract what the monkey had just said.

"Great," Keith muttered. "Another monster."

It was getting dark now, and the wind was picking up, howling through the pass and chilling him to the bone. Keith's fingers were starting to grow numb, and he suspected that if he stayed the night, he might not survive until morning. His suspicions were confirmed when a message flashed across his vision.

You are freezing: -1 HP per second until your body temperature rises

"Ouch," Bob said as soon as he dismissed the message. "Looks like you were just slapped with a debuff. Basically, any negative status, like the 'bleed' you got hit with during the battle or the 'stun' the ripper got, is considered a debuff, and let me tell you, it can get a lot worse than this."

The roar echoed through the pass again as Keith neared the top of the hill. He wondered if he would need to fight as soon as he reached the top. He really hoped not. His regeneration was managing to keep his HP at full, but if he got into a fight, it wouldn't recover until he was warm again.

However, as he crested the hill and the world below opened up, he was greeted by a completely unexpected sight.

The path continued, only this time, it moved downward, the area opening up. Further down, the hill flattened out to reveal a settlement, built inside what looked to be a crater of some sort. It was surrounded by natural stone walls covered in moss and vegetation. However, it wasn't the settlement itself that had grabbed his attention, but rather, the fight going on just a few dozen yards downhill.

The ground flattened as the pass opened up, and there, fighting in a spot with around thirty feet of space between the walls of the pass was a group of five people. They were all dressed strangely, wearing bizarre-looking armor and some carrying weapons that looked to be so large that no one would be able to wield them effectively.

They were up against the monster they'd been following, and Keith was more than glad to not have had to face this thing on his own, or at all, for that matter.

Analyze.

Shield-Wing Ripper
Level: 11
HP: 1,106/3,200

The creature was significantly larger than the ripper he'd faced, though it had the same talon-like claws as the previous monster. However, that was where the similarities ended. Its hide appeared to be made of stone-like scales, a row of black spines running down from the crest of its head to the tip of its tail.

A single, oversized wing sprouted from its back, and it was using it just like a shield, defending against attacks while using its razor-sharp claws to strike at anything within range. Its head was distinctly lizard-like, with the same red eyes as the previous monster and a mouth full of sharp teeth.

"Is this thing a ripper too?" Keith asked, ducking down and watching the fight.

His time to complete the quest was running out, but until this fight was over, he couldn't pass.

"The term ripper is used to describe an entire species of monster, including multiple sub-species," Bob said. "Anything with those talon-like claws and red eyes falls under that classification.

The good news is that most rippers can't use magic, though they can be a pain to kill and are extremely aggressive. They'll attack anything that moves, so if you see one, you're assuredly in for a fight."

Keith continued watching the battle as a broad woman carrying a truly massive sword shouted orders.

"Neil, I need that wing to come down! Tash, where's my snare? Hinge, stop being so useless!"

A man wearing a hooded blue cloak and carrying a twisted, bone staff made a sour face at the woman, then extended said staff. A blue crystal at the tip began to glow, and a moment later, a jagged bolt of ice shot from it, slamming into the monster's hide and shaving off a small amount of health.

"Woah," Keith breathed. "Was that magic?"

"Yeah," Bob said, seeming bored. "Looks like a standard Ice Bolt spell. You've seen one, you've seen them all."

"You've never seen one," Keith retorted.

"I have up here," Bob replied, tapping his furry temple. "That's what really counts."

Another woman – Tash, Keith presumed – lunged forward, hurling a glowing green net at the monster's feet as soon as Hinge used his spell. The net immediately tangled the monster's claws, and misty sparkles of light began floating up to surround the creature's head.

"Standard practice for monster hunting," Bob commented. "Someone distracts the monster, then a net is deployed. This one seems to have a tranquilizing effect. Next, one of them will try opening its guard..."

Bob trailed off as the monster staggered, shaking its head. The moment it did, another man – likely Neil – charged in, swinging a massive hammer and slamming it into the tip of the wing. A fine spray of dust shot into the air as the wing was knocked aside, more HP being shaved away from the bar above the monster's head.

"And now the big one goes in for the final blow," Bob said.

The woman in charge hefted her massive sword, swinging it up and around as a red glow ignited across the edge. With a yell, she bought it down, cleaving through the monster's spine and knocking its HP down into the red.

"What did she just do?" Keith asked.

"Used up a whole bunch of stamina for a big attack," Bob said. "Bad luck on her part that she didn't manage to kill it. They're pretty much doomed. If they'd had a fifth fighter – like they should – this would be over."

Keith's brows came down as he analyzed the situation from a tactical standpoint. Four fighters. One distracts, one traps, one clears, and one attacks. If there had been a second attacker – perhaps a nimble fighter who could strike multiple times – they could finish the monster. However, as he watched, the net finally broke, and all hell broke loose along with it.

The ripper roared, its claws shredding through the net. The trapper tried to move in with another, but its tail lashed out, catching her in the gut and slamming her into the side of the mountain pass. Keith winced as her head cracked against the wall, and she slid down, lying ominously still.

The magic caster ran over to help her, instead of staying to fight, leaving the two with unwieldy weapons to try taking on the much faster monster.

"They're going to be slaughtered," Keith muttered, watching as Neil only managed a partial block of the talon-like claws with the haft of his hammer.

A shout of pain echoed through the pass as blood sprayed from the deep puncture wounds, the man staggering back and tripping over the loose stones underfoot.

"I think you might be able to slip past now," Bob said. "The monster will likely be distracted by its meal, which gives you the chance to escape."

It was quite cold of the monkey to suggest a tactic like that, but regardless, Keith knew it was a sound one. He didn't stand a chance against this monster, so it was the best course of action. Still, the idea of just leaving these people here to die didn't sit well with him. He'd never been the type to simply stand by, not back on Earth, and not in any of the other worlds where he'd been sent.

"Here's to hoping my active skills can actually do something," Keith muttered as he began to run.

"Hey, Keith," Bob said, sounding a bit nervous. "You're not going to do what I think you're going to do, are you?"

Keith continued running down the slope, headed directly for the monster, whose back was currently to them as it tried to decapitate the leader.

"Oh, come *on*," Bob whined. "I thought you were smarter than this!"

Keith leaped into the air as he approached the monster, triggering his first active skill as he did, the momentum from his run continuing to carry him forward, and landed neatly on the monster's back.

7

The monster apparently didn't even feel him land, as it continued trying to crush the woman with the sword, who was currently using it to fend off the ripper's razor-sharp claws.

Keith took a moment to gain his balance, his feet scrabbling across the monster's back as it lunged. His skin had taken on a grayish hue, Stonestance having cloaked his body in a layer of stone.

"Why are we up here?" Bob moaned as Keith found what he'd been looking for and punched downward.

-5, Critical

The ripper let out a roar as Keith punched the spot on its back where the woman's sword had struck earlier. The monster bucked then, and Keith was thrown clear off, hitting the ground back-first and rolling over his shoulder to regain his feet.

He'd taken a small amount of damage in the fall, but thanks to his Stoneskin, it hadn't been much. Still, he had the freezing debuff, so his HP wouldn't regenerate. Worse, he'd barely done any damage to the monster, despite landing a critical hit.

"Any ideas?" Keith asked as the monster whirled on him, gleaming red eyes practically glowing in rage.

It was only when he got no answer that he realized that Bob was gone. He didn't have time to look around as the monster lunged toward him. Keith tried to move back, but he wasn't nearly fast enough to avoid being hit.

Luckily, it seemed that the people he'd come to save felt obligated to return the favor. As the monster lunged, Neil came charging in, and with a roar, slammed his hammer into the side of the monster's head.

The ripper's health dropped again until there was just a small sliver remaining but somehow managed to cling to life.

"Have you lost your mind?" Neil yelled, whirling on him. "You could have been killed!"

Keith responded by tackling him around the knees and knocking him to the ground. It was just in time, as the heavy tail swept through the spot where the man had been standing just a moment ago.

"You're welcome," Keith said, leaping to his feet and grabbing a rock as he did.

He hated having to keep relying on ranged weapons, but at the moment, the leader was pinned once more and was now taking heavy damage as the ripper tore at her with its claws.

The stone whipped from his hand, slamming into the side of the monster's head and doing next to nothing.

-2

The monster turned, glaring at him, but this time, the leader took advantage of the distraction. With a yell, she hoisted the massive sword over her head and brought it down on the monster's leg.

With a sickening *crunch*, the blade bit deep, blood spraying out in a fountain and coating her upper body. The monster's HP hit zero, and before it could so much as whimper, it dropped to the ground, dead.

Shield-Wing Ripper dies.

+75 XP

Keith was surprised to see that message, as he had barely done anything to the monster at all.

"Yeah, you might not have helped much, but you helped enough for the system to reward you," Bob said, hopping onto his shoulder.

"Nice of you to join me," Keith grumbled.

"Hey, I'm not a fighter," the monkey said with a shrug. "When you fight, I run. I'm a coward and proud of it."

"Thank you for having our backs," the leader said, coming around the monster and wiping blood off her face. "You might not have done much, but that distraction probably saved all our hides."

Up close, Keith could see how massive this woman truly was. Well over six-and-a-half feet, she towered over his own five-foot-ten-inches. She was also broad, her wide shoulders covered by pieces of bone armor.

Her skin was a dark tan, her black hair pulled back into braids, and her face was craggy and weathered.

"Happy to help," Keith said, taking the woman's extended hand.

"My name's Betty," the woman said, all but crushing his hand. "That sourpuss you saved is Neil, and the two over by the wall are Hinge and Tash."

"I'm Keith," Keith said, hiding a wince as she released his hand. "The monkey is Bob, my guide."

"I'm the brains of this operation," Bob said, puffing out his chest.

Betty laughed, reaching down and hauling Neil to his feet. The man still looked quite sour. Apparently, talking monkeys were common enough that no one thought anything of it.

"Are your friends going to be alright?" Keith asked, looking to the magic-user and trapper by the wall.

"Tash took a nasty blow, but she'll be fine once we get her back to the guild."

"Guild?" Keith asked.

Betty reached into thin air and removed a glowing green vial, then proceeded to pour it down her throat. Her wounds began visibly healing, the numerous cuts and gouges in her skin knitting back together.

"Yeah, we're all part of a guild," Betty said as Neil headed over to the monster's corpse, likely to loot it. "If I may be so rude as to ask, what are you doing all the way out here dressed like that and all alone?"

"I'm not from around here," Keith answered.

"Ah, an otherworlder," Betty said. "Makes sense. When did you arrive?"

"Nearly five hours ago now," Keith said, checking the time on his quest. "I really need to reach the town, though. I have a quest to complete."

"Say no more," Betty said. "Seeing as you helped us, the least we can do is escort you to Oster's Keep. We'll even give you an introduction at the guild. After what you did, they'll be more than happy to have you, and we're always recruiting."

The monster's corpse vanished, and Neil straightened to his full height. Keith noticed him holding a small green vial as well, which he assumed was some sort of healing item.

"Oy! Hinge! Make sure she makes it back in one piece, or I'll have your spleen on a pike," Betty yelled, making the magic-user cringe.

She then turned back to Keith, motioning him to follow her, then took off at a run. For someone so massive, Betty was quite nimble, and Keith soon found himself having a hard time keeping up. Thankfully, she realized this and slowed to match his pace.

"What kind of guild are you in, exactly?" Keith asked, needing to know more information about this group before he even considered joining.

There was always strength in numbers, and he knew his chances of survival would increase exponentially if he made some friends, but he didn't want to fall in with the wrong crowd.

"Our guild was founded to combat the rising monster population some thirty years ago," Betty said. "Since then, three more branches have opened across the continent. We also have rangers stationed on the others, our oldest and most experienced charting what has never before been charted. We're explorers, adventurers, treasure hunters, and an all-around insane group of individuals. In short, we hunt monsters."

Keith could see how monster hunting could be lucrative, at least in the way of gaining levels and experience. He hadn't suspected that there was an entire guild dedicated to something like this, though.

"How many members do you have?" Keith asked.

"In the Oster's Keep branch, we have around a hundred and fifty," Betty replied. "Membership includes free room and board, as well as discounted rates by our in-house blacksmith, alchemist, and bar. Additionally, we have a great selection of Class trainers, as well as Dungeons under our jurisdiction for training.

"We also have a constant stream of jobs coming in, which tend to pay quite well. The monster population is only rising, which means we can charge a premium for our services."

"You sound like you're really trying to sell me on this," Keith said. "What's in it for you?"

Betty grinned unashamedly.

"A five-silver finder's fee if you sign up and pass the entry test," she replied.

"I'll have to think about it," Keith said.

"I'm sure seeing it in person will help with that decision," the woman said. "And a personal introduction from me will definitely help your case, especially when I tell them how crazy you are!"

The woman roared with laughter, as though charging a monster several levels above his own had been funny. For some reason, Keith found that he rather liked this woman and found himself smiling right along with her.

Neil ran ahead, apparently having lost patience with their speed, reaching the town far before them. However, it didn't take the two of them long to reach the gate – a small opening cut into the stone.

"Looks like we made it just in time," Bob said as they walked through the surprisingly thick stone tunnel and emerged at the top of a flight of stone stairs, leading down and into the town proper.

*Congratulations! You have completed the quest: **Civilization***

+50 XP

+5 Bronze coins

Skill: Ranger has reached Advanced level III

8

"Wow, this place is amazing!" Keith said, looking around the small town as Betty led him through the darkened streets.

The actual town was set some fifteen feet down from the entrance, the two of them having walked down a flight of stairs carved into the side of the crater.

Lanterns were already being lit, residents leaning out of their open front doors to kindle the small wicks within. People moved about the hard-packed streets as well, either going home after a hard day of work or heading to the tavern to relax and drink.

All of the homes were built of stone and arranged in neat rows. The construction was solid, which spoke volumes about whoever was in charge of this small town.

In the many worlds he'd visited, Keith had noticed a distinct lack of planning in a lot of the smaller villages and towns. Things were typically built in a haphazard manner, with people crowding closer together than was strictly necessary.

Homes were also shoddy for the most part, people simply wanting a roof over their heads rather than taking the time to build a proper home.

"We're currently in the area of the town where living quarters are arranged," Betty explained. "Here, those who work for the town are allowed to rent these homes from Lord Oster. I should tell you that he and the guild master have an agreement that anyone who joins the guild doesn't have to pay any taxes, as our service is vital to keeping this town safe and prosperous. The others need to pay a five percent tax to the Lord every month on all wages earned."

"Yet another incentive to join the guild, I see," Keith said as more lights shone up ahead.

They exited the narrow street and walked into an open plaza, one that was ringed by a series of buildings and wooden carts. The carts had all been covered for the night, though the buildings were lit up, with people moving in and around them.

The most popular had a wooden sign outside, with a picture of a mug of beer painted on both sides. Another one had a picture of a bed, and a third building's depicted a sack bulging with items.

They were all pretty self-explanatory, and in a world where Keith suspected there were very few literate people, it likely made sense.

After all, the system always spoke in his mind, despite the fact that he could read the messages as well.

"Come on, this way," Betty said, placing a hand on his shoulder and steering him down another street.

This one was noticeably better, having been cobbled with actual stone instead of hard-packed dirt. Additionally, the houses here looked larger and better fortified. They continued down this street, finally emerging into a second plaza, though now there were two archways built to lead deeper into the town.

One was gated and guarded by several burly-looking fighters that were giving anyone who approached the stink eye. Looking further in, Keith could see a large manor, hidden amongst the numerous trees that had been planted there.

"The lord's manor, I take it," Keith said, pointing to the manor in question.

"Yup," Betty said. "He wanted to make sure the guild was close by, but not so close that he couldn't have his privacy."

She gestured to the second archway, over which was placed a sign of a roaring monster with a bleached white skull mounted atop it. This sign had words on it, which was a stark difference to the rest of the town.

Pest Control Guild

"Pest control?" Keith asked, raising an eyebrow.

"Marj has a weird sense of humor," Betty said, moving toward the archway.

"Marj?" Keith asked.

"Our guild master," Betty explained. "You'll meet him soon enough."

Keith followed the woman through the archway and found himself surrounded by trees. These had clearly been transported and planted here, though, as there didn't seem to be many of them in the area. After just half a minute of walking, the trees stopped, opening up into the single-largest structure Keith had yet to see in this world.

"Pretty impressive, right?" Betty asked as she headed to the open entrance, from which a loud swell of sound could be heard. "Come on!" she called as Keith hesitated. "Don't be shy."

Shrugging to himself, Keith followed the woman, a blast of warmth hitting him as he entered. Almost immediately, his debuff vanished and his health stopped flickering.

"She wasn't kidding about this place," Keith muttered, stopping for a moment to take it all in.

The building was huge and made up of two open floors. To either side of him, two sets of wooden stairs curved up to the second level, where he could see tables and chairs set up. The smell of cooking food assaulted his senses, reminding him of how hungry he was.

Ahead, he could see a bar, placed against the left wall, where several patrons sat, drinking from wooden mugs. On the right, he could see a counter, where several people stood in line, apparently waiting their turn. Above the counter was an image of a crossed yellow and green vial, with 'Alchemist' written over it.

A red glow appeared a bit farther down, and he could see an image of a hammer and anvil where the word 'Blacksmith' was written.

"Come," Betty called. "I don't want anyone else snatching you up before I bring you to Marj."

She grabbed his hand, all but dragging him through the crowded room toward the back, where a group of people sat around a curved table.

"Hey, Betty. Long time-!" said a man with a bright smile and sweeping brown hair, trying to intercept them.

Betty punched him in the face, knocking the man flat without even breaking her stride. Raucous laughter greeted this display as the man popped back to his feet, still grinning.

"I might have deserved that, but I hardly think it's fair of you to keep ignoring me," he called after her.

"Who was that?" Bob asked.

"My brother," Betty replied.

"Strange," Bob said. "I thought siblings were supposed to look alike."

The monkey wasn't very subtle in the way he phrased it, but Betty didn't seem to mind.

"He's a half-brother. As you can probably tell, I'm a demi-human. Kyle is completely human."

Keith, in fact, had not been able to tell that Betty wasn't entirely human, but that was likely due to the fact that he hadn't tried to analyze her.

Name: Betty
Race: Demi-human
Class: Swordbasher
Level: 10

Keith could have kept going – it seemed that his skill would give him all the information he desired – but it was at that moment that they reached the table.

"Betty," a gruff-sounding voice said. "Neil tells me you bagged a shield-wing. Good work."

"That I did," Betty said, her back straightening. "I also brought you someone, a potential recruit."

Betty then stepped to the side, finally allowing Keith a good view of the man at the head of the table. He was quite massive as well, just about as large as Betty herself, though he looked like he'd taken to smashing rocks with his face.

The man had long white hair which hung down his back in a loose pony. One eye was milky white, a series of scars crisscrossing his mess of a face. His nose was squished, and his bare chin had a piece missing from it.

"I know I'm not much to look at," the old man said with a wicked grin. "But I'm still here, while every monster I ever faced is in the ground."

"Not *every* monster," said a man sitting to his right with gray-streaked black hair.

"That's not important right now," the guild master said. "We need to make a good first impression if we want to keep recruiting. Or have you not noticed that our batch of newcomers is decreasing?"

Keith took the opportunity to analyze the man and was not disappointed by what he saw.

Name: Marj the Legendary Butcher
Race: Human

Class: Gravedigger
Level: 65

"What kind of monster is he?" Keith whispered out of the side of his mouth.

"A very old one," Bob replied. "He's got a title and a legendary class! We need to get you one of those."

"Don't mind Rufus," Marj said, turning back to Keith with a rueful smile. "He can be a bit pessimistic sometimes. Anyway, I hear you want to join the guild."

"I said I'd think about it," Keith said, looking to Betty. "Though Betty has been trying to sell me pretty hard."

"He'd make a great addition," Betty said shamelessly. "He jumped on a level eleven monster without hesitating for a second. If not for him, we'd have lost at least one of our fighters."

"Is that so?" Marj asked, looking at him appraisingly.

Keith felt suddenly uncomfortable and knew they were analyzing him.

"Only level three and no skills of which to speak," Marj said, his brows coming down. "You seem a bit old to be so weak. Didn't your parents help you level? Even a commoner with no class should be level five or six by your age."

Keith was a bit surprised that the man couldn't see any of his skills. As far as he knew, there shouldn't be anything interfering with others seeing who he was and what he could do. He'd need to ask Bob about this when they were done.

"He's an otherworlder," Betty jumped in. "Arrived only a few hours ago."

Now Marj seemed really interested.

"Level three in just a few hours, huh? Alright, I've decided. I want you to join my guild," Marj said, slamming his hand down on the table. "But first, you'll need to pass a little test."

A light *ping* sounded in Keith's head, and a moment later, a new quest appeared.

*Quest Available: **Initiation***
Marj has invited you to join the Pest Control Guild, but you need to pass a test first. Knowing them, you're probably going to have to kill something. Go figure.

Difficulty: C
Rewards: 100 XP, 2 silver coins, Membership in the Pest Control Guild

"Speak to Cragg to start your initiation," Marj said. "On my end, I hope you succeed. We could use more members with an actual spine!"

The man let out a bark of laughter, then turned to speak with Betty. Clearly, he was done with him, so Keith turned to leave.

"We'll catch up later," Betty said, grabbing his attention before he could go. "I hope you decide to stay. If you do, I'll buy you a drink for saving all our hides."

Keith nodded, then headed away. He was already mostly convinced – the perks sounded too good to pass up – but he needed Bob's opinion before he accepted the quest. He headed to a quiet corner, leaning against the wall and observing the room as a whole.

"So, what do you think?" he asked the monkey perched on his shoulder.

"You could do worse," Bob said with a shrug. "They laid things out pretty clearly. Joining the guild will mean having a lot of perks, especially when it comes to hunting monsters, and seeing as you have a world-level difficulty quest involving monster hunting, it's a pretty good bet that these will be the people to have backing you."

"What are the downsides, though?" Keith asked. "All of this has to come with some conditions attached, right?"

"Any organization you join will have some of those," Bob said. "For this guild, you'll have to join in on any guild-wide raids if you meet the level requirements. Additionally, you'll probably need to defend this town from any monster attacks, and should the guild itself be attacked, you'll obviously need to pitch in.

"On top of that, you'll be branded with a guild tag, meaning that any enemies of this guild will attack you on sight. But, considering what this guild does, I'd say you'd be getting more good than bad if you join up. Most guilds would try locking you down to a specific region or city, but this one is very far-ranging. Also, you'll be able to propose expeditions to new areas once you reach a specific rank within the guild."

"Rank?" Keith asked.

"Have you noticed the colored chains everyone here seems to have bound to their belts?"

"Yeah," he replied.

He'd noticed them but hadn't thought much of it.

"They each represent a rank within the guild. In fact, this is the standard accepted rankings across all guilds on every continent, so if you see someone with a high ranking, you can assume they're powerful, even if you can't see their status. In order, they're copper, iron, steel, gold, platinum, electrum, orichalcum, mithril, and adamantite.

"The first few are pretty easy to identify, and although you might think steel, platinum and electrum would all look the same, they can be easily identified. Steel will appear as a dull silver, platinum will be bright, and electrum will have a yellow tinge.

"Orichalcum will be green, mithril, blue, and adamantite, a dark, almost black, gray. I don't think I need to tell you this, but you probably don't want to start up with anyone above copper right now."

Betty had had a steel chain, while the others on her team had iron. Keith was sure Marj would have a high ranking, but the man was sitting the entire time and hadn't been able to see.

"Why wasn't Marj able to see my skills?" he asked, still curious about the strange occurrence.

"You have a master-level skill," Bob replied. "Only those with a grandmaster analyze skill or higher will be able to see your real skills. Anyone else who tries will see exactly what they expect of you, which is one of the more interesting parts of the system."

"I'm sure Marj has to have at least one master-level skill," Keith replied. "So why could I see his information?"

Strictly speaking, Keith hadn't actually tried to see the man's skills, but he got the feeling that he could have, had he wanted to.

"You have the Discerning Eye, one that is much more powerful than a simple analyze skill. Speaking of, it would probably be a good idea not to go blabbing about your skill levels to anyone. A level three with two master skills and several advanced skills is very much *not* common. People might see you as a threat and try to kill you, and as I've mentioned before..."

"If I die, you die," finished Keith with a sigh – the monkey had been very clear on that.

Still, it was a good thing to know.

"Well, I guess my mind's made up then," he said, pushing himself off the wall. "Let's go find this Cragg and get this quest underway."

9

Finding Cragg wasn't all that difficult, seeing as the man with a gold chain around his waist was literally standing on a table and roaring to the room at large about the guild initiation quest.

"I'm guessing that not everyone in here is part of the guild," Keith said, noticing that several people walking by were not wearing chains.

"The Guild makes money in more ways than one," Bob replied. "The blacksmith, alchemist, and bar owner offer discounted rates for guild members, but regular people come here too. Seeing as this is the only place in town to offer such a wide range of services, the guildhall is a good place to come if you need a specialty item that's not offered in the town."

"You there!" Cragg roared as Keith approached the table. "Have you come to take part in the quest to join our guild?"

The man spoke far too loudly, even for this place. He was dressed in heavy-looking armor that once again seemed to be made out of leather and bone, though it was of a type Keith had never seen.

Cragg was relatively short when compared with a lot of the others here, which was likely why he was up on the table. He had a long black beard, woven with beads, and a wild mane of hair spilling down his back. A massive, double-handed ax sat slung across his back, and strangely enough, Keith felt that this suited him.

Name: Cragg the Immovable
Race: Half-Dwarf
Class: Ax Maniac
Level: 26

"Yup," Keith said after doing a quick inspection of the man. "Marj offered me a quest and told me to come speak with you to begin."

"Excellent!" the man roared, making Keith jump. "I've still got to gather some more of these louts, so we'll all be meeting at the guild entrance in an hour and a half. Until then, I recommend that you visit the blacksmith and alchemist. Those rags you're wearing won't do you any good where we're going. You might also want to get some food in you. You look famished!"

"Are all dwarves so loud?" Keith asked Bob, wiggling a finger in his ear as he headed over to the blacksmith.

"No," Bob replied. "He's only a half-dwarf. Regular dwarves are much louder."

"Why did he and the guild master both have something after their names?" Keith asked as he got onto the line before the blacksmith's booth.

"It's called a title," Bob said, starting to pick things from his chest and eat them. "I think I mentioned it earlier. It's basically something awarded by the system when you do something amazing, like killing a legendary monster or clearing a special quest."

"What exactly does a title do?" Keith asked as they moved up one spot in line.

"Every title is different," the monkey replied. "But generally, they all add either a unique skill, permanent buff, or something similar."

"I take it that a buff is a positive effect?" Keith asked.

Bob nodded.

"Just as there are debuffs that harm, there are buffs that strengthen. Generally speaking, eating really good food or taking the proper potion before going into battle can make the difference between life and death."

"So, Cragg's suggestion to eat?"

"It's probably one you should take," Bob replied. "Also, I'm famished. A long day of running and hiding is really hard on my paws."

Keith decided not to reply to that comment. The monkey did give useful information, even if he *was* a total coward.

"Speaking of fighting, I've been noticing that some of my attacks are critical, while others are not. What's the difference in damage between them?"

"A critical basically deals double-damage," Bob replied. "Hit a vulnerable spot, like a joint or an already damaged area, and you'll deal more damage."

"And a massive critical?" Keith asked.

"Double critical damage. If you hit a *really* vulnerable area, like the eye or back of a throat, or...well, you already know, don't you?"

The monkey shuddered, and Keith remembered what the system had said to him after hitting the first ripper he'd faced in a particular area.

They moved up another spot in line, and Keith realized something important.

"Will five bronze coins be enough to buy me anything?" he asked.

He knew what the currency was but didn't know how valuable his money would be. Since they were the lowest denomination of coin, he had to assume that what he had wasn't much.

"Normally, no," Bob said, picking at his little teeth. "The average salary in Raiah is a silver a week. Normal room and board at an average inn would be twenty-five bronze, and an average meal should cost you around seven.

"Weapons and armor are ridiculously expensive if you bring only money. After all, hunting monsters is a dangerous business, and anyone getting those materials would charge a premium when selling. But, seeing as you already have the materials you need, it'll only be a fee for the work. Plus, seeing as you only have low-quality ripper materials, I'd recommend selling the smith everything you don't use."

"Is that why you told me to loot the monster?" Keith asked, looking around once again. "Is everyone's armor made out of monster parts?"

"Weapons, armor, potions, you name it. Everything here will be made of monster parts. They're typically far easier to obtain and can sometimes be even more durable than metal. Of course, once you start crafting higher-grade weapons, armor, or potions – typically in the rare category and higher – the list of materials will include some metal. Oddly enough, it's much harder to find."

The person in front of Keith moved away, finally leaving him to approach the counter. A pretty girl stood behind the counter, contrary to his expectations of a smithy, and gave him a wide smile as he approached. Behind her, Keith could see an entire operation going on, though he couldn't hear anything.

"Why is it so quiet back there?" he asked, puzzled.

"This must be your first time here," the woman said, pointing to her right and left, where two glowing rods were attached to the wall. "They're sound dampening items," she explained. "Can't have this place constantly ringing with all the racket those brutes make back there."

"That's interesting," Keith replied, wondering what kind of utility these might serve if he were hunting monsters.

It was definitely something to think about. He would need to remember this for the future.

"I'm about to go on my initiation quest," he said. "Cragg told to come visit. My clothes aren't exactly suited for monster hunting."

The woman gave him a once-over, giving a sympathetic wince when she saw the shirt that had clearly been shredded by a monster's claws.

"You're definitely going to want some armor. Since you're going on the initiation quest, I won't charge you full price, but even with the guild discount of fifty percent, it's still not going to be cheap."

Though Keith had never done this before, he brought up his inventory for the first time, seeing the list of things he currently had stored there.

Inventory: 3 Ripper claws, 3 Ripper ribs, Ripper pelt, Ripper spine, 5 bronze coins

He removed all of the crafting items, analyzing one of the claws as he did.

Name: Ripper Claw
Crafting Material for weapons, armor, and potions
Quality: Common
Value: No less than 1 Silver & 20 Bronze

That was interesting, Keith thought. It seemed that the system was giving him a valuation for the claw but wasn't telling him a solid price, which meant he could likely haggle to get a better one.

"What kind of armor could you make with this?" he asked, spreading the items out on the counter.

The woman leaned forward, mentally taking stock of what he had.

"We can make you a single set of heavy ripper armor or a set of light ripper armor and ripper weapon. However, I do have to warn you that ripper-type monster parts can only make bladed weapons, nothing blunt. The total cost of construction will be fifty bronze."

"Can we see what the light and heavy sets of armor will look like?" Bob asked.

"Sure," the woman said with a smile, then made a gesture in the air.

A new screen popped up before him, showing the details of the armor.

Name: Ripper Armor - Light
Pieces: 3 (Shirt, Pants, Shoes)
Quality: Common
Armor: +3 (Shirt, Pants) +1 (Shoes)
Requirements: None
Restrictions: None
Value: 4 Silver

Name: Ripper Armor - Heavy
Pieces: 4 (Helm, Shirt, Pants, Boots)
Quality: Common
Armor: +6 (Shirt, Pants) +3 (Helm, Boots)
Requirements: 10 Strength
Restrictions: -10% Agility
Value: 6 Silver, 55 Bronze

After looking the two over, it was abundantly obvious which he should be taking. Sure, the heavy armor offered better protection, but it would hinder his movement and speed, which was the last thing he wanted.

"What exactly is the number next to how much armor this set offers?" Keith asked.

"Simple," Bob replied. "The number equals the amount of damage blocked before you take damage. So, if you have an armor score of three, and you take five damage, you'll only be hit for two. Take any damage at three or below, and you'll take no damage."

"So, in total, the light armor will ignore up to seven points of damage?" Keith asked, hoping he'd added it up correctly.

"Yup," Bob replied. "And the heavy armor will ignore up to eighteen."

That was a big difference. Remembering how much damage that level two ripper had dished out almost made Keith choose the heavy armor. However, in the end, he stuck with his first choice.

"I'll take a set of the light ripper armor," Keith finally said.

"Great," the woman said, grabbing one of the ribs, the pelt, and spine – apparently, claws weren't needed for armor. "What kind of weapon would you like us to make for you?"

"None," Keith replied, surprising the woman.

"You want to go out and hunt a monster with no weapons?" she asked, looking at him like he was completely insane.

"I'm more of a hand-to-hand fighter," Keith explained.

"That might work if you're fighting people, but against monsters?"

"He's stubborn that way," Bob said. "He'll come around eventually."

The woman looked dubious, and Keith had the feeling she was going to try convincing him again, so he preempted her by changing the subject.

"How much will you give me for the rest of the materials?" he asked.

Keith knew he was being stubborn, but in his defense, his martial arts skill was the highest of all his skills. Additionally, he had two active skills that would support his unarmed fighting, and once he had some armor, Keith would feel more confident in approaching a monster and be less afraid of being shredded to a bloody pulp.

The woman leaned forward, her eyes gleaming with obvious greed.

"Two silver for the claws and one for the ribs."

Keith knew she was trying to rip him off in a big way. Each of the ribs was worth no less than a silver and fifty bronze. He proposed a counter-offer.

"I *did* risk my life for these monster parts," he replied. "I think five silver for the claws and four silver and eighty bronze for the ribs sounds more fair."

"I have a business to run," the woman countered. "I would never make any money if I just gave it all away. How about four silver for the lot?"

Keith felt like he was wasting time, but he countered back with another offer. He'd needed to haggle quite a bit in other worlds. So much so that as part of his Discerning Eye skill, he could see the value of items. As part of his Tactician skill, he couldn't easily be deceived. It also helped that the system gave him a value for the items in question.

After nearly ten minutes of this, they settled on a final amount. He would receive one silver and thirty bronze for the claws, and two silver coins each for the ribs, for a total of seven silver and ninety bronze. He paid her the fifty bronze cost to craft the armor, and she told him to return in an hour to pick it up.

He'd been worried that it wouldn't be ready in time, but apparently, the process was pretty quick.

"So, where to now?" Keith asked as he moved his remaining seven silver and forty bronze into his inventory.

"The alchemist," Bob said, his stomach letting out a loud gurgle. "Then to get food."

10

"Should I have saved any of those materials for the alchemist instead of selling them?" Keith asked as he got onto the much shorter line for the next shop.

"Nah," Bob said, rubbing his stomach. "If you'd had anything useful, I'd have told you to save it. The only ripper part you had that would have been useful was the spine, but since you needed it for the armor, you were better off selling the rest."

"What can I do for you, dear?" the elderly woman at the counter asked as they moved up to the counter.

"We're looking for some potions," Bob said. "We're about to go out on his initiation quest, and Cragg sent us here."

"Of course," the woman said with a motherly smile. "Here's my list of recommended potions for first-time monster hunters."

Another screen appeared before them, with a list of options.

Name: Weak Healing Potion
Quality: Common
Effect: Restores 50 HP
Value: 2 Silver

Name: Weak Stamina Potion
Quality: Common
Effect: Restores 50 STA
Value: 2 Silver

Name: Middling Armor Potion
Quality: Uncommon
Effect: +50 Armor for 60 Seconds
Value: 5 Silver, 70 Bronze

Name: Weak Recovery Potion
Quality: Common
Effect: Restores 100 HP Over 30 Seconds
Value: 3 Silver, 50 Bronze

"This stuff is expensive," Keith groaned.

With the exception of the Armor potion, these seemed to be the lowest-quality ones as well. He could hardly imagine how expensive higher-quality ones would be. Additionally, the fact that the price was fixed gave him a good indication that there would be no haggling here.

"The monster parts needed to procure these potions are expensive," the woman said, still smiling benevolently.

"Do these prices reflect the guild discount?" Keith asked hopefully.

"No," the woman replied. "Only guild members receive the discount."

"But I'm going for my initiation," Keith replied. "Isn't that good enough?"

"I'm afraid not, dearie," the woman said, her voice taking on a hard edge. "Now, are you going to buy anything or not? I have customers waiting."

Okay, Keith thought. *Don't piss off the old lady.*

"How much *is* the discount for those in the guild?" Keith asked.

"Fifty percent is the standard," the woman replied. "Now, if you're not going to buy anything..."

"I'll buy a healing potion," Keith said, pulling two silver coins from his inventory.

It pained him to do so, but it would pain him even more if he were killed due to wanting to save a bit of money. It was important for him to keep reminding himself what he was fighting for. If he succeeded in this world, his parents would be brought back, and his family would live a happy life together.

If he died, his siblings would still have a good life, but it would be a life without him or his parents.

"Excellent," the woman said, smiling brightly once more as she took his money.

She reached into thin air and removed a glass vial with a glowing green liquid within. Keith took it, analyzing it, just in case she tried to rip him off. However, all he saw was what she had promised, a weak healing potion that would restore 50 HP. With his total health at 80, this could be the difference between life and death.

"Let's get some food!" Bob cheered, raising both his paws in the air.

"The food better be cheaper than the potions," Keith muttered.

No one liked being ripped off, and this single potion had cost him over a quarter of what he'd made selling the monster parts. He now only had five silver and forty bronze remaining, and if they tried charging an exorbitant fee for a meal, he decided he would go hungry.

"Guild members eat for free here," a burly man with a stained apron said when he approached one of the dozen or so food counters on the upstairs floor of the guild. "Since you're heading out on the quest, you'll either join the guild after or die trying, so the least I can do is give you a free meal!"

The man roared with laughter, as though this was the funniest joke he'd ever heard, then plopped a platter on the counter. It contained an entire roast chicken, a mug of something fizzy, and a pile of fruit that could have killed someone if they tried eating it all.

"Enjoy," the man said as Keith headed to a table.

"Why does everyone believe me when I tell them about the quest?" he asked as he sat down.

Bob immediately leaped off his shoulder, snagging a piece of blue-colored melon and taking a big bite.

"Lying about a quest is impossible," the monkey said as the juice dyed the fur on his chin. "The system would penalize you if you did, so you'd be smart not to."

"Good to know," Keith replied, then, like the monkey, dug into the food.

It wasn't the best he'd ever had – he'd eaten some truly fantastic dishes over the course of his many lifetimes – but it certainly wasn't the worst either. It was hearty and filling, which was what anyone would want out of a meal before going to hunt monsters. To his delight, a message flashed before his eyes as he finished.

You are satiated: +10% HP & STA regen, +50% cold resistance.

"Nice!" Keith said, pumping his fist in the air.

"That's not bad," Bob replied, apparently having seen the message as well. "But there's much better food available. Once we join the guild, you should get options to choose your meals. Then we'll really get some good bonuses."

There were still about thirty minutes left before the armor would be ready and about forty-five before the quest began, so Keith took the time to explore the building, seeing what they had to offer.

He tried to ask about class trainers but was told that only those in the guild had access to them, meaning that if he wanted the bonuses that came along with a class, he would need to wait until after the quest was completed.

Aside from the blacksmith and alchemist, there was also a small shop where survival gear and rations were sold. Keith didn't need to be prompted to make several purchases here, including a rope, canteen, warm cloak, rations to last a week, and a sleeping roll in case he had to rough it.

Altogether, this purchase cost him his remaining bronze and another three silver coins, leaving him with just two to his name. Still, he viewed these purchases as essential. Oddly enough, the most expensive item was the cloak, though after viewing its properties, it was easy to see why.

Name: Woven Cloak
Quality: Common
Effect: Immunity from Cold-type Debuffs
Value: 2 Silver

"I think your armor is just about ready," Bob said as Keith examined the cloak, feeling the rough material between his fingers and frowning.

It was unfortunate that it wasn't soft, but it would keep him warm, and he likely wouldn't feel it through the armor anyway.

"Yeah, I think you're right," Keith replied.

He'd learned to keep time without the aid of a watch or clock centuries ago, so he had a pretty accurate grasp on the time that had passed.

Together, they headed to the blacksmith, where they picked up the armor. Keith examined it, quite liking the design, though it did appear a tad barbaric. The spine had been used for the back of the shirt, and the rib had been split into a thin frame, over which part of the hide was stretched.

The pants were made almost entirely of the hide, as were the shoes, though there were slivers of bone protecting his shins and knees, as well as the top of his shoes. Overall, it seemed quite sturdy and warm. From what he'd seen so far, that would be important.

"Come on," Keith said, heading to the restroom. "I think I need to change, and I should have just enough time to sit on the porcelain throne before the quest starts."

Unfortunately, the thrones in this world seemed to be made of wood – not that he was surprised. Fortunately, though, they *did* have a version of indoor plumbing, which had not been the case in the last couple of worlds he'd visited.

"Too bad I can't just use the system to equip the armor," Keith said as he exited the bathroom.

It had only taken a couple of minutes to don the armor, but it had been a pain to do so in the small stall.

"You'll get a room of your own once you pass the quest," Bob said as Keith threw the cloak around his shoulders and hooked the metal clasps into the protruding bones on his armor.

"Nice to see that the blacksmith here is competent," Keith said, tugging on the cloak a couple of times and not feeling it budge.

He couldn't count the number of times that simple things like a cloak clasp had been overlooked, leaving him to have to tie it around his neck or drape it ineffectually over his shoulders.

"Good! You look ready to go," Cragg roared as Keith approached the entrance.

There were two other people already waiting with him as well, a man appearing to be in his early twenties and a tall woman with red-streaked black hair, around the same age. The man had a pair of daggers thrust into his belt, while the woman carried a white bone scythe slung across her back.

"No weapons?" Cragg asked after looking him over.

"I fight with my hands," Keith repeated.

"Your funeral," Cragg replied with a shrug.

He was still speaking way too loudly, but Keith was getting used to it.

"The quest is simple," Cragg said, turning to address the three of them. "There's a nasty basher that's been skulking around the outskirts of the town. The three of you will track it down, and kill it, then bring back its head as proof! Do this, and you're in."

*Quest available: **Sneaky Basher***
A basher-type monster has been skulking around Oster's Keep. Hunt it down and kill it, then bring back its head. Good luck with that.
Difficulty: C
Rewards: 200 XP, 5 silver coins, Monster Hunter skill

Completing this quest will automatically complete the quest: **Initiation*

Accept? Yes/No

Keith mentally said *yes*, and the quest was accepted.

"Excellent," Cragg boomed. "Try not to die!"

With that said, he turned around and disappeared into the crowd, leaving the three of them alone.

"Why do I have two quests for the same mission?" Keith asked, curious.

"It happens sometimes," Bob replied. "Lucky you. You'll get rewarded twice, though you'll need to collect one reward from Marj and the other from Cragg."

"The system won't reward me?" Keith asked.

"Since these quests were handed to you by people instead of the system, they're required to give you the rewards."

"I take it that you're new to this world?" the man on his team asked, getting Keith's attention.

"Yeah," Keith said, giving him a rueful smile. "Is it that obvious?"

"Yes," the man replied, returning the smile in kind. "Name's Jared, and this is Cayla. We both traveled here from Rooster's Keep in the east."

"You're not using a weapon?" Cayla asked, frowning slightly.

Keith noticed a small fang poking from her top lip as she did and only then noticed the abnormally pale skin and too-bright green eyes that seemed to glow.

Name: Cayla
Race: Vampire
Class: None
Level: 6

"I'm a martial artist," Keith said. "I fight bare-handed."

"I know you're not from this world," the woman said. "But you won't get far trying to fight monsters without a weapon."

"So people keep telling me," he grumbled. "Look, if it makes you feel better, I'll look into something once this quest is over. I've already survived two monster encounters and didn't even have armor when I did. I think I can survive a monster hunt with two people who have my back."

"That's the spirit," Jared said with a grin. "I *like* him."

"You like everyone," Cayla said.

"And you don't like anyone," Jared replied easily.

"That's because people don't like me," Cayla retorted. "I'm fine around humans, but a single look at me and they're pulling out their warding charms and garlic like I'm going to eat them or something."

"To be fair, you are a vampire," Jared said, turning and heading out the door.

"A vampire who has a bloodring," the woman retorted, lifting a pale hand to reveal a crimson ring on her index finger.

"Bloodring?" Keith asked in an undertone while Jared and Cayla continued bickering.

"Vampires need to drink human blood to survive," Bob said. "That's why they're generally feared on this continent. However, several decades ago, Guzzlarian the Glutton created the bloodring. In short, it suppresses the vampire's bloodlust and allows them to survive by eating normal food.

"The Royal Guild gives them out for free, as vampires are good to have around. They tend to get racial bonuses to melee classes, and having powerful fighters in their debt is something the Royal Guild seems to like."

"Guzzlarian the Glutton?" Keith asked, trying not to laugh.

"The most powerful alchemist in the world," Bob replied. "A Sage."

Ridiculous name aside, the man was extremely powerful. After creating an item like the Bloodring, he was likely to be influential as well. Keith would make sure to keep that in mind for the future.

"Hey, slowpoke, try and keep up," Jared called, making Keith realize that he'd been lagging behind.

He sped up, mentally kicking himself for getting so distracted. He was just happy he hadn't allowed it to happen in the field. Out there, even the smallest mistake could cost you your life, as he had discovered many times in the past.

11

"So," Jared said as they exited the town, finding themselves facing a darkened landscape. "Anyone know how to track a monster?"

They'd exited on the opposite side of where they'd entered, so Keith was facing new terrain. They were still surrounded by mountains, but now, tall pines began popping up here and there, and the ground was a bit softer. When Cayla didn't say anything, Keith decided to step forward.

"I can track," he said. "Though I'm not very good at it."

"Good enough for me," Jared said. "I'm terrible at tracking, and for some bizarre reason, so is Cayla."

The woman's cheeks grew a bit red at that, but she didn't say anything to defend herself.

"Come on then," Keith said, taking the lead.

It felt strange, ordering these two around, especially seeing as Cayla was a higher level than him and Jared was likely to be the same. Still, with as much experience as he had commanding on the battlefield, he fell naturally into the role.

He slowly circled east, feeling the cold nipping at his cheeks and his breath steaming in the air. The cloak kept him warm and protected him from cold-related debuffs, but it didn't do much to stop him from feeling the cold on the parts of his body it didn't cover, like his face.

"How are you not bothered by this cold?" Keith asked, turning his head to the other two.

"We're used to it," Jared said with a shrug. "The weather is constantly cold here in the north. Even in the summer, it never really goes much above about fifty degrees."

"Do they use the same unit of measurement for temperature as I did back home?" Keith asked his guide in a lowered voice.

Come to think of it, he'd been understanding people perfectly this entire time, which was a bit strange. The language barrier had been a big issue until he learned to identify the patterns in languages. Still, adjusting to a new world had always been a matter of years, not hours.

"The system is doing all that for you," Bob replied. "With so many people from different cultures, races, and even worlds ending up in Raiah, no one would be able to understand anything if left to their own devices. The system actively works to translate everything that anyone says into a way you will understand.

"To you, they are speaking English and using a measurement of temperature you understand. But to them, you are speaking Raianese. It's all very complicated, which makes me happy that I don't need to think about it."

"That monkey of yours is smart," Jared said, butting in on their conversation. "Where can I get a guide like that?"

"I have a name, you know," Bob said, turning to glare at the man. "And I am not an object to be won. I am a world guide and one of a kind!"

"There are quests that allow you to get your hands on one," Cayla said with a sigh. "But you'd actually need to stumble into one, as only the system can give them out. The best places to find them would be in dungeons or on unique quests."

"I'm sure we'll run into plenty of those in this guild," Jared said brightly.

"Why exactly did the two of you come to join up?" Keith asked.

"Adventure and glory!" Jared exclaimed.

"They're the only guild that would have me," Cayla said with a shrug. "How about you?"

"They're the first guild I came across," Keith said, also shrugging. "I liked what I heard, so I decided to accept the quest."

"That's the spirit," Jared said loudly. "Diving into adventure headfirst. That's so manly!"

Keith was about to reply when he felt a chill run down his spine. A flash of purple caught the corner of his eye, and he turned, spotting a shallow imprint in the hard-packed ground a few yards away.

"I think I found something," he said, turning and heading away from the wall.

It seemed his Discerning Eye skill was even better than he'd thought. He'd only realized the track was there on a subconscious level, but the skill had then made him notice it. He would need to work on raising this up more, as it seemed to have many uses.

"Good eye," Jared said. "I'm impressed."

"I wouldn't have seen that," Cayla grudgingly admitted as Keith stooped to examine the track.

It was a rounded circle, with four smaller imprints set up as a square. Looking up, Keith could see the tracks continuing, outlined in clear purple and giving him a direction to follow.

"What type of monster is a basher?" Keith asked, deciding to get some actual information this time.

"Basher-types are about as dangerous as rippers," Bob said. "However, instead of being fast and vicious, they're slow and need a bit more instigating to rile up. The difference is their armor. While rippers are known for their massive damage-dealing capabilities, bashers are much harder to kill. They also deal crushing damage and can break bones more easily."

Keith didn't like what he was hearing. While the monster they were hunting would deal less damage, broken bones were far more dangerous than a few cuts by his estimation. Additionally, a tougher monster meant a longer fight, which meant more chances to become injured.

The sky began to darken as they followed the trail, and thunder rumbled overhead. Keith began to move a bit faster as the first freezing drop of rain hit his nose, not wanting the trail to be washed away.

It only began raining in earnest once they were under the cover of the pines, and by that point, the towering trees were protecting the trail.

Signs of the monster's passing were becoming quite apparent now, with broken branches, patches of missing bark, and deeper gouges in the ground. Keith even found a few small stone chips, which Bob told him to put in his inventory.

"They're stone scales," Bob explained, "which tells me that this will be one of the scaled-type bashers, which is a good thing. The plate-armor-type bashers are much harder to kill."

"I think we found our monster," Keith said, having to speak up over the rain.

"Where?" Jared asked as he and Cayla stopped next to Keith beneath the branches of a tall pine as they tried to stay out of the rain for even a few seconds more.

"There." Keith pointed to a massive boulder sticking out from between the trees.

It was covered in moss and slick from the rain. It overhung a bit though, leaving a dry area within. It was pretty dark out by now, thanks to the cloud cover, but Keith could see some movement, and when he squinted, he was able to analyze the monster.

Stone-Quake Basher
Level: 8
HP: 1,800/1,800

"It's called a stone-quake basher, and it's level eight," he continued. "It's got a massive health pool, though. A thousand-eight-hundred."

Jared winced as Cayla pulled a glowing orb from her inventory.

"What's that?" Keith asked, squinting against the light.

"An illuminator," Cayla said. "Albeit a weak one. It'll last about fifteen minutes, and I've only got one, so we won't be able to take our time with it."

"I've also got one," Jared said. "But I'd rather not have to use it."

"Cheapskate," Cayla muttered.

"What's an illuminator?" Keith asked.

"Just watch," Bob said.

Cayla squeezed the white orb in her hand until Keith thought it would burst. Then, with a loud pop, the sphere turned a pale blue and the light increased exponentially. Cayla then cocked her arm back and hurled it upward.

It reached the top of its trajectory some twenty feet up, and strangely enough, remained lodged there, shedding light over the entire surrounding area.

"Remind me to buy a few of those when we return," Keith said, realizing how useful an item this would be.

With the illuminator in the sky, he could clearly see the basher. It was around fifteen feet long and covered in black and tan stone scales. It reminded him of a massive lizard, albeit one with club-like feet and a head that resembled an anvil.

Small, beady black eyes appraised them, the monster narrowing them in displeasure. It clearly didn't want to get up, though it did utter a threatening growl as they approached.

"Bashers are weak in the underbelly, eyes, and mouth," Jared said, reading from a small book he'd pulled from his inventory. "Don't try striking the sides, as it will do practically nothing, and avoid the legs and tail at all costs unless you're using a blunt weapon."

"Where did you get that?" Keith asked as the man tucked the book away and drew his daggers.

"Picked it up at the guild," Jared said. "It wasn't cheap. Even this basic book on monster lore cost me two small gold bars."

Keith recoiled at the massive cost of such an item. That was the equivalent of two-hundred silver coins. Where had he gotten all that money?

"I could have told you that," Bob muttered. "No need to go wasting money on an expensive book when you've got me."

"So, how are we doing this?" Cayla asked, drawing her scythe.

Keith analyzed their situation with a practiced eye. He had centuries of combat experience, and now that he had a team with him *and* didn't need to charge in without a plan, he could think things through. He leaned into his Tactician skill to see what it could do.

Purple lines appeared, tracing their way from them to the monster as phantoms of themselves began attacking. He visualized the fight from several different angles before he came up with the best solution.

"As far as I can see," Keith said, "the first thing we need to do is pull that monster out of its shelter, or we'll only be able to attack from one direction. I believe I have the best chance of not being hit, so I'll try luring it out. Once I have, Jared will move to the underbelly, while Cayla will move in to take my spot and hold its attention."

"And what will you do once I do that?" Cayla asked.

Keith grinned at that, a dangerous smile that had sent many enemies fleeing in terror.

"I'm going to kill the monster, of course."

12

"Are you *sure* this is a good idea?" Bob asked as Keith ran at the monster, cloak billowing out behind him.

"It's the best we currently have," Keith replied, his feet slapping the ground and sending up sprays of freezing water each time he did.

"Good luck then," Bob said, then leaped off his shoulder, snagging one of the nearby tree branches and disappearing from view.

True to his nature, the coward had run away to hide as soon as the fight began, but Keith had already expected as much, so he wasn't surprised.

The basher let out a snort as Keith circled around to its head and followed up with another threatening roar. Clearly, it didn't want to have to deal with them right now. It was cold and wet, and the monster had a nice dry spot to wait out the storm.

Keith dashed right at the monster's head, then used his Stonestance. His stamina bar dipped by twenty, and his skin took on a grayish hue. He locked his legs as he neared the monster, but he continued sliding forward, carried by the slick ground underfoot. Keith used this momentum to turn into a kick, his toughened leg slamming into the monster's nose.

-12

Keith shoved back, leaping out of the way and avoiding the monster's mouth as it lunged forward to bite him, its stony teeth slamming shut on empty air. Letting out a breath, he charged back in, halted for an instant to allow the monster to lunge, then spun around its head and drove an elbow into its eye.

-16

Unfortunately, the monster seemed quite capable of protecting its weak points, as it instinctively blinked, closing a stony eyelid right as his elbow impacted. The force of the blow barely budged the monster, but it seemed to aggravate it a bit.

Keith stepped back until he was pressed up against the sloping stone. The monster turned its head and lunged, and Keith spun to the side. There was a loud *crack* as the anvil-like head of the monster slammed into the wall, and Keith was gratified to see its health bar dip a bit more.

Still, despite that, the monster still didn't seem motivated enough to stand, as it just lifted a hammer-like leg and swiped at him. True to Bob's information, the monster was slow, so even a level three fighter like Keith could easily dodge the clumsy attack.

The basher rumbled out another roar as Keith moved in to attack again. His Stonestance wore off as he moved, so he decided to see what his Brutal Rain could do. In his mind, it sounded like an ordinary skill, something he could do on his own, but Bob hadn't led him astray thus far.

His skill was activated, and his stamina fell by forty this time, but as soon as it activated, Keith could see that it had been well worth it.

His body was immediately outlined in a crackling blue light, and he lunged forward. He felt strength surging through his limbs as he delivered a crushing punch to the basher's closed eye.

-34

There was a loud *crack* as a line appeared in the stony lid, a dark brown fluid leaking out from the crack.

The monster roared in pain this time and reared upward, slamming its head into the top of the lip. Keith continued moving, his body feeling like it needed to burn through the energy he'd just lent it.

With the basher having reared, it gave him a perfect shot at its pale underbelly, all of which was glowing purple, indicating a weak spot. Additionally, there was a spot of darker purple further down.

I'm not going to do it, am I? Keith asked himself.

His body moved as though of its own volition, and he unleashed three more brutal punches, committing himself to the course of action.

-106, Massive Critical

-110, Massive Critical

-128, Massive Critical

*Stone-Quake Basher will never have children again. What kind of monster **are** you? Do you have no **shame** or **mercy**?*

Stone-Quake Basher is Enraged, and I don't blame him!

The crackling blue light faded from around his body as soon as the fourth punch landed, and Keith retreated from beneath the rock as the basher screamed in pain.

I'm really going to need to ask Bob about these strange messages from the system, Keith thought as he gave himself a moment to breathe.

He didn't know what 'enraged' would mean practically, but he got the feeling that he'd successfully gotten the monster's attention, as it rolled to its feet, eyes blazing in anger and locked right on him. With a roar, the monster charged out from under the rock, tail carving a deep groove in the wall as it did and showing him just how dangerous it was.

Going to want to avoid being hit by that.

"Now!" Keith yelled, hoping the others could hear him.

On cue, Jared and Cayla charged from within the cover of the trees, and Keith did his best to avoid being squished by the enraged monster. Jared got into position quickly, slashing at its underbelly and dishing out a nice amount of damage.

To his surprise, the man wasn't doing nearly as much as he had just a few minutes ago. He was then reminded of his many skills that added a good deal to his overall damage output.

"Come on, rocky," he called, taunting the monster. "You couldn't hit me if you tried!"

He had no idea if it would work, but he figured it couldn't hurt. The monster roared, then lowered its head and tried to ram him. Its head slammed into the ground as it charged, tearing up a furrow in the earth and sending a small mountain of dirt and stone flowing toward him rapidly.

Keith remained right where he was, taunting the monster. At the last second, he dove out of the way, though not quickly enough to avoid any damage at all.

-19 damage

Keith landed flat on his stomach, his legs having been caught by the mountain of dirt. However, the monster itself suddenly stopped, its charge arrested by the tree that it slammed into. There was an ominous cracking sound, followed by a loud groan.

A moment later, one of the tall pines slowly toppled back, only falling a few feet before its branches got tangled up in the other trees.

"You're completely insane, aren't you?" Cayla exclaimed as he finally reached him.

"Only a little," Keith said, taking her proffered hand and getting back to his feet.

His legs twinged a bit, but aside from that, he felt that he should still be okay to run. The monster, oddly enough, hadn't sustained any damage from that charge – Keith suspected that the dirt had cushioned it enough to avoid it completely. However, its HP continued dropping as Jared slashed away at its stomach.

"Keep its attention," he said as he turned to run. "I'll call for you when I'm ready."

He didn't give Cayla the time to ask questions, just turning and running back toward the stone that the basher had been taking shelter under. Freezing rain streamed down his face, trickling down the back of his shirt and sending chills spreading all over his body.

Thankfully, the cloak seemed to have some sort of waterproof component, as it didn't become heavy and waterlogged, instead shedding rain and keeping him mostly dry.

He could hear the sounds of the monster's roars, the thumping of its heavy footfalls, and the splashing of water as it sprayed into the air. He skidded to a halt beneath the overhang, the rain immediately stopping as he did.

"Looks like you finally came to your senses," Bob said, appearing from seemingly nowhere. "Hiding while others are fighting for their lives is a completely underrated art form."

"You mind telling me what a monster being enraged means?" Keith asked as his eyes roamed over the stone.

"The monster's damage output doubles," Bob replied. "But it will focus completely on attacking and not bother with defense, so the damage it takes will double as well."

"Good to know," Keith replied, finally finding a spot that looked promising, then focusing on the stone as hard as he could.

For a moment, he was afraid that it wouldn't work, but after a few seconds, purple light flared across the face of the boulder, several darker spots standing out.

With a grin, Keith activated Stonestance and struck the nearest spot. The blow sent a shockwave up his arm to his shoulder, but he barely noticed it as stone dust flew in the air. He planted his feet, then pivoted on his back leg, twisted his hips, and leaned into the blow.

The second punch slammed into the stone with a loud *crack*. When he removed his fist, a thin line spread across the face of the stone. Keith grinned once more, then moved to the next spot.

He was forced to use Stonestance several more times, even having to remove his stamina potion when he nearly ran out. He didn't have the luxury of just waiting to recover it naturally, as his companions were fighting for their lives.

He looked back every few seconds to check on how they were doing. Cayla was currently keeping the monster's attention, just as they'd planned. She did this by staying in front of it, her scythe constantly moving in glittering arcs, reflecting the light of the illuminator hanging in the sky above.

She was barely doing any damage at all, but each time the tip of the scythe would slam into the monster's nose, it assured that the basher's attention remained on her and not on the man underneath, who was actually doing damage.

By the time Keith reached the final spot, the basher's HP was down to about half, which was impressive, considering its massive health pool. Still, with three people fighting it, the amount of health became slightly less daunting.

"While I think it's quite obvious what you're planning, I do have to know how you're going to get the monster to come this way," Bob said as Keith's fist slammed into the last dark purple spot on the stone.

An ominous rumbling went through the rock as a line appeared, spreading across its entire length. Keith dodged out from beneath it, watching the stone carefully and hoping that he hadn't accidentally gone too far.

Thankfully, the rumbling stopped after a few seconds, and the cracks stopped forming.

"I don't think it'll be too difficult to get that monster's attention," Keith said. "After all, I *am* the one who got it enraged."

Taking a deep breath of the freezing air, Keith shouted with all his might.

"Cayla! Bring the monster this way!"

The woman started, obviously having heard him, and began to try running around the monster to do as he said. The plan was underway. He just hoped that his preparations had been enough and that things would work out as he planned.

13

As soon as the basher caught sight of him, Cayla disappeared from its thoughts. With a roar that shook the ground, the monster charged, picking up speed to the point where Jared was forced to dive out from beneath it or be trampled.

Keith stood absolutely still, waving his arms and trying to be as noticeable as possible. Rain sheeted off the basher's stone scales, flowing to the ground in dozens of rivulets as the monster charged. Each time it landed, the ground shook slightly, the heavy monster leaving deep footprints in the rain-softened ground.

"Almost there," Keith muttered, slowly beginning to back up.

The others must have seen what he was planning by now, but by this point, the basher had built up enough speed that they wouldn't be able to catch up.

"Be careful!" Cayla yelled. "If it hits you, you're as good as dead!"

There was no need for her to tell him that. At this point, the basher was moving with the equivalent force of an eighteen-wheeler driving thirty miles per hour. If that thing hit him, it would bowl him right over, then turn his body to paste as it continued its charge.

Stone teeth gleamed in the illuminator's light as the basher opened its mouth wide and roared once more. Keith took another step back, his body tensing. The basher lowered its head and sped up even more, charging over the last few yards with all the force it could muster.

The instant it took its eyes off him, Keith ran for all he was worth. His stamina was already low from all of the uses of Stonestance, and it plummeted further as he ran. His eyes remained glued to the bar as it dropped past ten, then down to five. With all his remaining strength, Keith threw himself forward as his stamina hit zero, his body suddenly losing all strength.

He hit the ground, unable to move. It was the most frightening thing that had ever happened to him. He was conscious and well able to understand what was happening, and yet, his limbs refused to obey him, his body remaining frozen, paralyzed on the freezing, wet ground, as his stamina slowly began to refill.

There was a roar, followed by a shuddering crash that he could feel reverberate through the earth, as the basher presumably made contact with the weakened stone wall. Although he couldn't see, Keith could picture the monster running past him and slamming into the wall.

An ominous groaning sound echoed through the air, followed by several loud *cracks*. There was a snuffling roar, and the ground shook as the stone shelf collapsed on top of the monster. Several loud *thuds* followed, along with a roar that turned into a high-pitched whine.

Hands seized Keith beneath his arms, hauling him to his feet.

"Took you long enough to get here," Keith panted, still finding his body uncooperative.

"Someone should have warned you about running out of stamina," Cayla said, pulling his arm over her shoulder.

"Why can't I move?" Keith said, staring at the pile of rubble and the monster, who was still alive.

"If you run out of stamina, you're basically paralyzed until you recover it completely," Jared said. "For the record, by the way, that was epic! You should have seen how that monster went down."

He looked to Cayla, who smiled wryly.

"Yeah, I can agree with that. It looks like your plan worked pretty well."

"Not well enough apparently," he said, as the monster began to stir, a single, beady eye opening to glare at the three of them.

Dark blood streamed over its face, its head having miraculously avoided being crushed by the falling boulders. A quick examination showed that its HP was in the yellow, about three-quarters of the way gone.

As it shifted, slowly pulling free from the slabs of rock, its health dropped a bit more, and the bar turned red.

"How much time do we have?" Cayla asked, still backing up.

Keith watched the monster for a few seconds, calculating how long it would take for it to escape.

"Ten seconds at the most."

His eyes flicked to his own stamina bar, which was only around half full.

"It's going to take me about sixty to be able to move again."

"We won't be able to avoid that monster if we have to drag you along," Jared said, his voice sounding suddenly somber. "Someone will need to buy some time."

"Don't be stupid," Cayla said, but it was too late.

Keith's left side slumped, forcing Cayla to take his entire weight as Jared ducked out from under him.

"Keep moving back," Jared called as he ran at the monster, drawing his daggers.

"Come back here!" Cayla screamed, sounding panicked.

"Listen to her," Keith yelled. "Don't try to play hero!"

Jared reached the monster and attacked, his daggers tracing a series of lines across the monster's craggy face.

The basher roared, then lunged, causing the rocks to shift once more. A large slab fell, landing on its tail. A loud series of *crunches* and *cracks* followed as the stone scales broke and dark blood welled up, only to be immediately washed away by the falling rain.

Cayla paused as she watched, holding her breath, and Keith had to prompt her to keep moving back. Jared was doing alright for now, but there was no way he'd be able to hold out for the full time needed.

"I'm going to help," Cayla finally said when the monster tried biting Jared's face and missed by about an inch. "Sorry about this."

Keith didn't have time to protest as he dropped him back to the ground. Thankfully, he landed on his stomach, facing toward the monster. It was why he got a great view when the basher finally broke free of the trap, its anvil-like head catching Jared in the gut and tossing him into the air.

Blood flew from the man's lips, the daggers falling from limp fingers. Cayla let out a scream as he hit the ground, his eyes having rolled up in his head. His armor around the area of impact had been very obviously damaged, and judging by the way his chest rose and fell, he had broken several ribs.

Keith silently cursed, his eyes flicking back to his stamina bar as it hit 115/130. Another fifteen seconds, and he'd be able to move again. Cayla just needed to hold out until then.

With a scream of rage, the woman leaped to her feet, drawing her scythe and charging directly at the monster. The only reason she wasn't immediately killed was due to the fact that the monster was injured. Massive chunks were missing from its hide, its scales having been shattered completely in some places, revealing a pale skin beneath, glistening with blood and rain. Its tail hung limp, dragging on the ground behind it, while it was noticeably favoring its right side.

The edge of Cayla's scythe glowed red as she swung at the monster's face. It reared back, causing her to simply clip its chin, missing any weak points and causing her to overbalance. The basher came down, trying to hit her with its chin, but she managed to turn her stumble into a clumsy roll.

However, in the process, she lost her scythe, and when the monster shifted, it stepped on the weapon. With a loud *crunch*, the haft shattered, leaving the woman all but defenseless.

"And that's why I don't want to use a weapon," Keith muttered as his stamina topped out.

Strength flooded back into his limbs as he sprang to his feet, the use of his body returning to full functionality. Even as he ran at the monster, shouting and waving his arms, he silently swore to never allow his stamina to run out again. He ran past the unconscious Jared, glad to see the man still breathing, and focused on the monster before him.

Thankfully, it still seemed to remember who had been responsible for neutering it and turned its attention away from Cayla as she tried to scramble out from beneath it. The basher began to move forward at a lumbering walk, roaring all the while.

Dark blood leaked from between its jaws, flowing down its legs and coating its hide. This monster was on the brink of death. All he had to do was hit it hard enough to kill it.

Keith charged the basher, angling to its right, which was already weakened. The basher tried to turn, placing too much weight on its injured leg, and with a half-roar half-squeal, it toppled onto its side.

Keith reached the monster just as it fell, his Advanced Tactician skill having told him exactly where its head would end up.

He used his Brutal Rain, and blue light crackled across his skin as overwhelming energy coursed through his body. He lunged, throwing a hard punch at its eye, his fist slapping wetly into the closed lid.

-22

The second and third punch landed in quick succession, the monster having to keep its eye closed to avoid taking a critical hit.

-22

-26

On the third blow, a loud crack echoed in the air as the eyelid finally split. Reflexively, the monster's eye flashed open as it let out a roar of pain. Keith didn't hesitate, putting all of his strength into the final blow.

His fist struck the glassy eyeball, then sunk into the monster's skull.

-130, Massive Critical

Stone-Quake Basher is blinded in one eye.

Keith waited to see the message that would tell him the monster was dead, but when it didn't come, he grew worried. He tried to pull back but found his arm stuck fast in the monster's skull. He didn't allow himself to panic, quickly lifting a leg and placing it on the monster's chin for better leverage.

The monster kicked, throwing him off balance. He fell, his arm twisting at an awkward angle as pain flared through the limb.

-44 damage

Your arm is broken: HP capped at 90% until healed.

Keith gritted his teeth against the pain, struggling to get his legs back under him. The basher moved, yanking him to the side, sending pain flaring through his broken arm as it dragged him across the ground.

-16 damage

Keith's HP dropped dangerously low, and he knew that if something wasn't done soon, he would end up dead – again. Without conscious thought, he pulled the healing potion from his inventory, ripped the cork out with his teeth, and downed it, restoring almost all of his lost health.

The basher moved again, but this time, help finally arrived.

"Sorry it took me so long," Cayla said, seizing his broken arm and yanking as hard as she could.

-6 damage

Keith's arm popped free, but Cayla's act of kindness cost her, as the basher – apparently too weak to stand – bucked its head back. One of the protruding points of its massive head caught her in the chest, knocking her off her feet and dropping her health by half.

Keith let out a breath, the air before him steaming as freezing rain began to numb his throbbing arm. A quick check of the monster's health told him that a single good attack would finish it for good.

"Stay down!" he shouted as Cayla tried to get to her feet. "It's blinded on that side. It won't be able to see you."

The monster's head twitched – apparently, its hearing was still fine – and threw itself toward him. It did this by kicking its legs, which shoved its prone body across the ground. Keith only just managed to get out of the way, cursing the monster's persistence.

In his experience, a wounded beast would often flee if the avenue permitted. Very rarely would an animal fight to the death when it didn't have to. This monster could have fled on multiple occasions, but every time, it had chosen to remain and fight. He just didn't get it. What would drive a monster like this to just keep fighting? Was that just how monsters in this world operated?

Keith dashed around the side of the monster's head, scooping up one of Jared's fallen daggers and once again cursing his need to use a weapon. With his right arm broken, he didn't like his chances of fighting this monster with just his hand.

It shifted once more as he skidded to a halt, his arm cocked back and waiting. He could hear the beating of his heart, rain sheeting down from above, pouring down his face and dripping from its chin.

The instant he saw the monster's beady, black eye, his arm whipped forward in a smooth motion, the dagger flashing through the air and burying itself deep in the basher's remaining eye.

-158, Massive Critical

Stone-Quake Basher dies.

+100 XP

14

Level Up!
Congratulations! You have reached level 4. You have 5 Stat Points to allocate.

Skill: Tactician has reached Advanced level V

Skill: Bladed Mastery has reached Advanced level X

Skill: Stonestance has reached Novice level VII

Skill: Brutal Rain has reached Novice level III

Keith dismissed the notifications, still staring at the dead monster, hardly believing it was dead. It lay there, rain pouring off its body, Jared's dagger still poking from its eye.

"I can't believe you did it," Cayla said, moving around the monster's body.

She was clearly in shock, but there was no time for that right now.

"Do you have any healing potions?" he asked, his eyes flicking to her own health, which was slowly recovering.

"I have a couple," she said.

"Good," Keith replied, steeling himself against the pain in his arm – it would have to wait until they got back to the guild. "Give it to Jared. I don't know how broken bones heal in this world, but I'm guessing they don't just fix themselves. In the meantime, I'll fetch the monster's head and loot the body, and then we'll head back."

Cayla nodded, then ran over to help Jared as Keith moved to loot the monster.

"How exactly are broken bones healed?" he asked as Bob hopped onto his good shoulder.

"You'll need to see a healer. Either that or buy a healing potion that also mends bones. Additionally, there are specific bone repair potions, but those are a lot rarer."

Keith placed his hand on the monster's corpse and thought the word 'loot.' Immediately, several messages popped up.

You have received: 22 Basher scales, 12 Basher spikes, 6 Basher stumps, Basher thumper & Basher head (Quest item)

"What the hell kind of body part is a thumper?" Keith asked as the monster's body vanished.

"You got a thumper?" Bob exclaimed. "You lucky such and such!"

"What?"

"The thumper is literally the rarest drop a basher-type monster can give you!"

"We're ready to head back," Cayla called, interrupting the excited monkey. "Did you grab the daggers?"

"We'll talk more when we get back," Keith said, stooping to grab one dagger.

The illuminator finally ran out at that point, and he had to rely on his Discerning Eye skill to find the other, but it didn't take too much longer.

"Cayla?" he called, trying to locate the woman.

"Here."

Her voice sounded off to his left, and after a few seconds, he found her.

"How's he doing?" Keith asked when he saw the man slung over her back.

"He's alive," Cayla said. "But unconscious. He should be fine once we get him to a healer. I just hope this won't be too expensive."

It took a bit longer to reach Oster's Keep, as they needed to navigate in the rain and keep a slower pace due to their injured companion. Still, the natural stone wall soon came into view, and thankfully, the guards at the gate didn't give them too much trouble.

"We need a healer," Keith called as he shoved the heavy door to the guildhall open.

He was sure they looked like a mess. After all, they were completely drenched, covered in blood, cradling broken limbs, and carrying a half-dead person.

However, after a few people turned to see what the commotion was about, they went back to their own business. Clearly, heavily-injured people were quite common around here.

"Out of the way! Move!"

Cragg, the overly loud half-dwarf, shoved his way through the crowd, followed by a small man dressed in tattered robes.

"Set him down over here," the man ordered.

Cayla complied, and Keith watched with interest as the healer held his hands out over the unconscious Jared. Green particles of light floated from his fingers, seeping into the man, and before their eyes, Jared began to recover.

His chest evened out, expanding to a normal size once more, and the pallid look vanished as his skin took on a healthy flush. His breathing eased, though the man didn't immediately regain consciousness as Keith had expected.

Jared's HP slowly ticked up until it was full, and only then did the healer turn to Keith.

"Come on. You next."

Keith didn't argue, stepping forward. Just as the earlier message had stated, his HP had stubbornly refused to fill all the way, thanks to his broken limb, and that was not to mention the actual pain he felt.

He let out a breath as a soothing warmth flooded into his limb. He felt something within shifting around, and a moment later, the pain stopped. His HP began to tick up as he flexed his fingers.

"Why did it take so much less time to heal me?" Keith asked after thanking the healer.

"Because your injuries were far less severe," the man replied. "Good work in getting him to me so quickly, by the way. Any longer, and he might not have recovered fully."

"Was the damage really that severe?" Keith asked.

"Several broken ribs, a punctured lung, and internal bleeding," the healer replied. "His HP was capped at 40%, and there was a debuff that would lower that cap every hour until he recovered. He was so bad that he had attracted the Potential Cripple debuff, which, as I said, would have left him with a permanent disability had he not been treated in time."

"I guess the final question is how much do we owe you?" Cayla asked, cutting in.

"Nothing," the healer replied. "The guild offers up to three complimentary healings a month. Since I take it that you completed your quest, I'll take this one off your credit. You *did* complete the quest, right?"

In answer, Keith pulled the basher head from his inventory, though he made sure to do it in a clear area. It was quite large – coming all the way up to Keith's chest – and grotesque, with both eyes missing and its stony tongue lolling out of the side. Strangely enough, no blood leaked onto the floor as Cragg let out a booming laugh.

"Alright, you've completed the quest! Welcome to the guild!"

*Congratulations! You have completed the quest: **Sneaky Basher**.*

+200 XP

Go to Cragg to collect the rest of your rewards.

*Congratulations! You have completed the quest: **Initiation**.*

+100 XP

Go to Marj to collect the rest of your rewards.

"Here you go!" Cragg boomed, removing a shiny copper chain from his inventory and having it to Keith, along with five silver coins.

He did the same for Cayla, though it seemed Jared would need to wait until he woke up to receive his rewards.

"And the final reward," the man boomed, extending a hand.

A window popped up before Keith, and he quickly read it over.

Skill available!

Monster Hunter
Level: Novice – I

You're a terrifying monster hunter. You hunt monsters. It's pretty self-explanatory...

+10% Damage

Keith readily accepted the skill, and another unexpected prompt flashed in his vision.

*Skill: **Monster Hunter** has advanced to Beginner.*

Monster Hunter
Level: Beginner - IV
You're a terrifying monster hunter. You're a little better at hunting monsters. It's pretty self-explanatory.
+20% Damage, +5% Armor piercing

Well, that was unexpected, Keith thought as he added the coins to his inventory and thanked Cragg for teaching him the skill. He wondered if the immediate advancement had something to do with his previous experience with hunting. It kind of made sense, but he would need to confirm with Bob once they were away from prying ears.

"Well, you now have access to all of the guild's amenities and discounts!" Cragg said. "Go to Aargh to get your housing straightened out. If you want any quests, just go check out the job board. See you around!"

Keith hid a wince as the man wandered away, presumably leaving someone else to take care of the monstrous head. He turned to Cayla, who was looking to the still-prone Jared worriedly.

"I'll get him to a bed," she said, moving to pick him up.

"Wait," Keith called. "The loot from the basher."

"Keep it," Cayla said. "You saved both our lives out there. I'm sure Jared would agree."

"If you're sure about that," Keith said, extending a hand with both daggers.

"I'm sure," Cayla said, giving him a strained smile. "I'll see you around, Keith. If you ever need someone for a quest, I'll be happy to join you, and while I can't speak for Jared on this matter, I'm sure he'd say the same."

Keith watched the two of them go, disappearing into the oddly crowded main floor of the guild before turning his attention to Bob.

"So, shall we go find Marj and get the rest of our reward, then go to bed?"

"Sounds good to me," Bob replied, drooping over his shoulder. "I'm pooped!"

15

"Good work killing that monster," Marj said, handing over two silver coins. "I'm sure you've got a bright future in our guild."

"Thank you," Keith said, hiding a yawn. "Do you know where I might find Aargh?" he asked, hesitating on the truly bizarre name.

"Aargh can be found on the second floor," Marj said, extending a finger upward. "There should be a sign with a key painted on it. Best to put that chain on before you go, as he won't even talk to anyone not in the guild."

Keith thought that was a rather strange thing, but seeing as the man's name seemed to be the sound people made when they were in pain, he wasn't going to question it.

Now seven silver coins and many monster parts richer, Keith headed up the stairs, already twining the thin copper chain through his belt. It wasn't hard to find the sign with the key, where a massive brute of a man wearing a much-too-small pair of glasses was reading a book.

"The Adventures of Bogo the Baboon?" Keith asked, getting the man's attention.

Aargh looked over the top of his book before closing it and placing it beneath the counter.

"New guild member, I take it?" he asked in a gruff voice.

"Yeah," Keith replied. "I'm looking for a place to sleep."

"Obviously," Aargh replied, pulling a copper-colored key from beneath the counter. "Copper rooms are through that door. Room number is on the key. If you lose it, it'll cost you ten silver to replace. So don't lose it."

With that said, the man took his book back out and proceeded to ignore him.

"Friendly guy," Keith muttered as he headed to the far side of the floor, where a rickety-looking door sat, hanging on a single hinge.

"Some people are just like that," Bob said as Keith pulled the squeaky door open.

He headed in, and the noise from outside mostly died down. The floorboards creaked underfoot as he walked down the narrow hallway until he reached a weathered door with the number *69* stamped on the front.

"Someone has a childish sense of humor," Keith said while he inserted the key into the lock.

"I don't get it," Bob said as the door swung open.

"So this is what Coppers get," Keith muttered, examining the room.

A single narrow bed was shoved up against one wall, and a small lantern sat atop a nightstand. Aside from that, the room was completely bare. Well, aside from the cobwebs that sat strung up in the corners.

"Yeah, I probably should have warned you about that," Bob said, sounding apologetic.

"What was all that about housing for guild members in town?" Keith asked, closing the door behind him.

He had to shove it extra hard for it to close, and the lock stuck a few times as he twisted it.

"I'm pretty sure you need to be at least a gold to get one of the houses on the outskirts. But you should get a more decent room if you become an iron."

"Oh, yeah? And how long will that take?" Keith asked, sitting down on the bed.

It made a horrible squealing noise as he did, as though he had just stabbed it in its nonexistent guts.

"It could happen tomorrow," Bob said with a shrug as Keith removed his cloak and put it back in his inventory. "It all depends on how strong they think you are. But realistically, you won't be promoted to iron until you either reach level ten or show that you have an intermediate skill, which in your case, would be suspicious."

Keith grunted as he lay down on the hard bed, deciding to leave his armor on. He'd slept in worse places, but seeing as he was still a stranger to this world, he would be a lot more comfortable sleeping in something that would offer some protection.

"Why was I rewarded both for killing the monster *and* completing the quest?" he asked, tucking his hands behind his head and staring up at the darkened ceiling.

"Bonus XP," Bob replied with a yawn. "You obviously didn't get as much XP as you would have, had you defeated the monster without taking the quest first. But you definitely got more XP in total due to having a quest in the first place. Even split three ways, you would have gotten 200 XP at most for beating a monster like that."

"Why, though?" Keith asked. "That monster was level eight, while I was at three."

"Your companions were higher-level, so the system would have awarded you based on their levels, not yours. Had you gone on that quest alone and lived, you probably would have gotten about 750 XP for defeating the monster alone, and likely another 1,000 between the two quests you got.

"However, the difficulty of the quest would most definitely have been A, which means your chances of survival would have been dismal at best."

"Yeah," Keith admitted without any sense of false pride. "I would have failed that quest without a shadow of a doubt if I'd had to go it alone. Better to take a smaller reward and live."

"I always knew you had common sense," Bob said, sounding half asleep.

"Go to sleep, Bob," Keith said. "We'll talk more in the morning."

A low snore was his reply.

Keith let out a long breath, then tried to relax in the uncomfortable bed as he pulled up his status and assigned his stat points – two to strength, two to vitality, and one to endurance – then looked over his status.

Status
Name: Keith
Race: Human
Class: None
Level: 4
XP: 300/400

HP: 100/100
MP: 0/0
STA: 140/140

Strength - 16 (14+2)
Vitality - 10 (8+2)
Endurance - 14 (13+1)
Agility - 13
Intelligence - 0
Wisdom - 12
Luck - 5

Skills

Passive
Bladed Mastery: Advanced – X
Ranged Mastery: Intermediate – IV
Martial Arts: Master – V
Peak Health: Advanced – VIII
Tactician: Advanced – IV
Quick Learner: Advanced – V
Ranger: Advanced – III
Punisher: Master – I
Discerning Eye: Advanced – VIII

Active
Stonestance: Novice - VII
Brutal Rain: Novice - III

Equipped Items

Armor
Light Ripper Shirt
Light Ripper Pants
Light Ripper Shoes

Total Armor Rating: 7

Weapons
None

He was close to level five already, and he'd only been here for roughly twelve hours. He had also almost died several times, but that seemed to be pretty standard for the worlds he'd lived in. The Trickster hadn't been lying when he'd said this world would be dangerous, and for some twisted reason, Keith had chosen one of the most dangerous guilds to join.

He grinned to himself as he closed his eyes. He had been a bit disappointed when he'd discovered this was a game-type world. Now, after spending just a few hours here, he was already starting to warm up to it.

He liked the idea of finding better gear, having better armor made, and yes, even finding a weapon – he had been forced to accept that reality after needing to use a weapon against the basher.

He could now understand why his brother had enjoyed gaming as much as he did and hoped to continue leveling up, finding new quests and items, and killing even larger and more dangerous monsters.

With this thought in mind, Keith curled up, dragging the thin blanket over his body and went to sleep. Tomorrow was another day, and he couldn't wait to see what it would bring.

16

"My back feels like it was trampled by a herd of angry preschoolers," Keith groaned as he stretched in his tiny room.

His breath steamed in the air, the cold having seeped in during the night, and his nose felt like it had been frostbitten. Still, oddly enough, he had no debuffs, and his HP remained full.

"I know what you mean," Bob complained, crooking his neck from one side to the other. "You are not a comfortable bed."

"No one asked you to sleep on me," Keith replied as he worked to loosen his tight muscles.

His stomach growled then, reminding him just how hungry he was, and Keith decided it would do better to warm up over a good breakfast.

"Let's go see what they've got available," he said, already imagining something steaming and hearty.

Bob leaped from the bed, landing on his shoulder as he opened the door, tail curling around his shoulder.

The hallway was just as cold as the room, but once he exited into the guildhall, the temperature noticeably rose. Judging by the lack of people in the hall and the dull sky outside, Keith estimated it was somewhere around six in the morning and that today would be an overcast day. He was used to getting up early, and despite not feeling well-rested due to the uncomfortable bed, Keith knew he wasn't going to be able to go back to sleep.

Thankfully, the cooks seemed to up, as delicious smells permeated the air. He headed over to the nearest counter, where a woman with blue-tinged skin and strange, webbed ears was reading a small pamphlet.

"Good morning," Keith said, giving her his best smile. "What's on the menu today?"

The woman craned her neck, looking down to his guild chain, then flicked a finger, throwing up a menu.

There weren't many options, and he ended up going with a hot cup of tea, a small loaf of brown bread and butter, and some eggs.

"So," Bob said, ripping a piece off his loaf and chewing slowly. "What's the plan for today?"

"I thought I'd look around for a class trainer," Keith replied, sipping his tea. "Do you have any suggestions?"

"I would suggest you pick a sword or bow-type class, but seeing as you're being stubborn about those, how about a blunt weapon-type class?"

"You mean like a staff or hammer?" Keith asked.

"Yeah, something like that," Bob replied. "This way, you can still dish out some damage but won't run the risk of getting it caught on anything."

Keith thought about it for a few moments, then nodded. He liked the idea of using a blunt weapon, and although he would need to start from the beginning, as he'd never used one before, it would still be better than using a bladed weapon.

"You might also consider carrying around a brace of daggers or something similar," Bob said. "And don't give me that look," he said, wagging a small finger at him. "You might have a higher Martial Arts skill, but I think we've already established that it doesn't work as well against monsters.

"That single dagger you threw did more damage than any attack you dished out during the quest. So, just as a backup, I would consider it."

"Fine," Keith sighed. "I'll consider it. Now, will you tell me what I can do with all the items I got from the basher?"

"Let's see what you've got," Bob said, then removed a single item of each from his inventory.

"I didn't know you could do that," Keith said, examining each of them.

"I have all permissions," Bob replied. "Unless you'd like to restrict me, I can do practically anything."

Keith didn't mind all that much. Bob's life was linked to his own, so it would only be detrimental to the monkey if he were to try harming him. Additionally, Bob provided so much useful information that Keith actually preferred it this way.

"Go on," Keith said as Bob opened a description of each.

Name: Basher Scale
Crafting Material for weapons, armor, and potions

Quality: Common
Value: No less than 1 Silver & 60 Bronze

Name: Basher Spike
Crafting Material for weapons, armor, and potions
Quality: Common
Value: No less than 2 Silver & 75 Bronze

Name: Basher Stump
Crafting Material for weapons, armor, potions, and other items
Quality: Common
Value: No less than 4 Silver

Name: Basher Thumper
Crafting Material for weapons
Quality: Rare
Value: No less than 2 Small Gold & 95 Silver

"Woah," Keith said, his eyes going wide as he read the description of the last item. "You mentioned the thumper was a rare find, but I had no idea how valuable it was."

The thumper was a round, knobby-looking thing some foot-and-a-half in diameter. It was gray and black, containing an almost stone-like appearance. The only part of it that wasn't round was the large hole on the bottom. Peering inside, he could see a glimmer of gold.

"Yeah," Bob said as he put the items back in his inventory. "As I said, the thumper is the rarest drop from an ordinary basher-class monster. They can only be used for weapons, so I'd recommend you hang onto it.

"As for the scales, they can be used for excellent armor, as well as armor potions. The spikes can be used for healing and stamina potions, as well as weapons, while the stumps can be used primarily as armor, but also for add-on items or jewelry."

"I take it the blacksmith and alchemist will be our fist stops today," Keith said.

"You take it right," Bob answered as he polished off the last of his bread.

Keith quickly drank down the rest of his tea, excited to get started.

You are satiated: +15% HP & STA regen. +65% cold resistance.

"I guess you were right about having better food for actual members," Keith said as he headed down the stairs.

"You're back," the woman at the blacksmith counter said. "And I see that you're officially part of the guild. Congrats!"

"Thanks," Keith said, looking past her to where several men worked. "Who exactly is the blacksmith?"

"My husband," the woman said, hooking a thumb over her shoulder to where a short, stout man was silently yelling at a terrified-looking youth with a smudged face. "The name's Sally, by the way, and you are?"

"Keith," he replied, turning his attention back to the woman. "I've actually got some new pieces I collected. Would you mind showing me what kind of armor you could make with these, as well as any stat-boosting items?"

Bob opened his inventory for him, pulling out all of the required items for new armor.

"Oh, now these are mighty more useful than ripper parts," the woman said, looking over the scales, spikes, and stumps.

"Just show him what light or medium armor he can have made," Bob said. "If you've got any hybrid armor available, we might be interested in that as well."

"Sorry," Sally said. "No hybrid armor will be available to you just yet. The lowest-quality hybrid armor we make has a requirement of twenty-five in the corresponding stat."

"What's hybrid armor?" Keith asked.

"Armor made from parts of more than just a single monster type," Bob replied. "But it looks like you'll need a stat above twenty-five to wear armor like that, at least of a type that they make here."

"Here are the models we can make for you using these materials," Sally said, and a new window popped up.

Name: Scaled Basher Armor – Light

Pieces: 3 (Shirt, Pants, Shoes)
Quality: Common
Armor: +5 (Shirt, Pants) +3 (Shoes)
Requirements: None
Restrictions: None
Value: 14 Silver, 20 Bronze

Name: Scaled Basher Armor – Medium
Pieces: 4 (Pauldron, Shirt, Pants, Boots)
Quality: Common
Armor: +7 (Shirt, Pants) +5 (Pauldron) +3 (Boots)
Requirements: 10 Strength
Restrictions: -8% Agility (None/w Str 15+)
Value: 26 Silver, 95 Bronze

Name: Spiked Basher Armor – Medium
Pieces: 4 (Helm, Shirt, Pants, Shoes)
Quality: Common
Armor: +6 (Shirt, Pants) +3 (Helm, Shoes)
Requirements: 10 Strength
Restrictions: -5% Agility (None/w Str 15+)
Value: 21 Silver

"I'd say that out of all the options, the medium scaled armor looks like the best option," Keith said after reading them over.

He had a strength above fifteen, so there would be no restrictions, and this armor would also give him the best coverage and defense boost.

"I agree," Bob said. "Though it will likely take more pieces of craft."

"Aye," Sally said. "The medium scaled armor will use eighteen scales and three stumps. It'll also cost you five silver coins to craft."

Keith winced at that number, but he looked to Bob, and the monkey nodded his head.

"Alright," he said, removing the required money from his inventory and handing it over.

"Excellent!" Sally said, taking the money and crafting materials required. "The armor will be ready in about an hour. Did you want to see anything else?"

"Yes," Bob replied. "Any items that can be crafted to boost stats, specifically vitality."

Sally drummed her fingers on the counter for a moment, looking between his remaining crafting materials and him.

"I only have one vitality-boosting item that would currently work for you, but you don't have all the required materials. You'd need three stumps and one eye. Unfortunately, seeing as basher eyes are one of the weak points, they're not often dropped upon death. So, if you want the item, it'll cost you one silver and seventy bronze to make."

"And if I'd had the eye?" Keith asked, already suspecting what the answer would be.

"Twenty-five bronze," the woman said, then added, "sorry."

"It's fine," Keith sighed. "Can I see the item?"

Name: Basher's Eye
Quality: Common
Item Type: Pendant
Effect: +2 Vitality
Value: 28 Silver, 45 Bronze

"What do you think?" he asked Bob.

"You can always sell the excess spikes and scales to the alchemist," Bob replied. "I'd tell you to take it. It might not be a huge boost, but an extra twenty points of health definitely couldn't hurt."

"Alright," he said, turning back to Sally. "I'll take it. Will you buy the ripper armor back from me once I get my new set?" he asked in a sudden bout of inspiration.

"We're always happy to buy weapons, armor, and items," Sally said. "But the condition will determine the price."

"Sounds good to me," he said, feeling a lot better about handing over more of his precious silver coins.

By the time he was done, the guild was starting to get a bit busier, so he headed over to the alchemist to get some more potions, and hopefully, some money.

17

"I think I'm okay with this," Keith said, checking on his inventory.

He'd picked up three stamina and healing potions at the alchemist, as well as a single armor potion. He'd sold the rest of the basher parts – with the exception of the thumper – and due to that, he'd even come away with a profit. He'd had seven silver coins and eighty bronze. After that, he'd gone to the shop and purchased two illuminators and a lantern, not wanting to run into another fight in the dark unprepared. Once his spending was complete, he had six silver and five bronze left.

"Yeah, I think you did alright," Bob replied. "And good on you for having the self-control not to sell the thumper."

Keith had to admit that he had been extremely tempted to do so, especially when he'd seen how much he could have gotten for it. Still, the idea of making some sort of blunt weapon with it convinced him to hold onto it for now.

"So, where do you think we can find a class trainer?" he asked, looking around the slowly filling guildhall.

"Beats me," Bob replied. "Why don't you ask around? I'm sure you'll be able to find someone."

That was exactly what Keith did. Before long, he was directed to several trainers who were sitting around the hall, but after speaking to four of them, he began to feel disheartened. They all taught classes that involved some sort of combination of a bladed weapon and only incorporated the blunt aspect.

For example, there were the Ax Maniac and Swordbasher classes. They both involved an absurd amount of strength, which he wasn't really sure he even wanted to use. His style involved strength, to be sure, but agility and endurance were equally as important.

"I don't know about this," Keith said as he approached an elderly woman who was sitting at a table on her own.

"She has a platinum chain," Bob said. "I'm sure she knows what she's doing."

The woman looked up as he approached, fixing him with bright blue eyes and a hard stare.

"Um, hi," Keith said, feeling a bit awkward. "I'm looking for a class that focuses on blunt weapons and was told you were one of the trainers."

"And what exactly do you have in mind, as far as your fighting style is concerned?" asked the woman.

"Well," Keith said, then let out a long breath, deciding to be completely upfront. "To be honest, I'd been hoping to fight barehanded. I've had bad experiences with bladed weapons, but after fighting a few monsters, I can see that I'm going to need a weapon, regardless of my preference. So, I figured something blunt would be a good alternative."

The woman shifted in her seat, now looking genuinely interested.

"Most people who join up generally want to swing around a great lump of a sword or an ax, something with prestige. Very rarely do I get people who are interested in learning from me. Do you know what class I offer?" she asked.

Keith shrugged.

"No idea," he replied. "But the last few trainers I've spoken to have all used some form of bladed weapon, with a blunt *aspect*. Not an actual blunt weapon."

The woman reached back, and with one hand, pulled a massive, two-handed hammer from her inventory and slammed it onto the table. Keith was expecting the table to buckle under the pressure, but it must have been quite solid, as the hammer didn't so much as scratch it.

"What I teach is called the hammerer class, one that focuses on pure, destructive power and the ability to crush anything in your path!" The woman grinned like an insane person when she said this, and Keith wondered what he'd just gotten himself into. "But," she continued, "from what you've been telling me, it sounds like you're looking for a hybrid class, something that will allow the use of a weapon while still capitalizing on the martial arts."

"Is there a class like that available?" Keith asked, becoming a bit excited.

"Kind of," the woman said. "Hybrid classes tend to be more powerful but require a few steps to obtain. In simpler terms, it's much easier to just accept a regular class, which is what most people want anyway. But, if you'd like, I can offer you a quest to get one."

Keith looked to Bob, who shrugged.

"Hybrid classes are difficult to obtain," the monkey said. "Which is why I didn't recommend one to you. But, if you're willing to put in the work and take the risk, I'd tell you to go for it. It's something that will cost you more upfront, but in the long-term, it will be to your benefit."

"I'm in," Keith said, feeling a bit of hope swelling in his chest. "What do I have to do?"

*Quest available: **The Road Less Traveled***
*You seem to like making things difficult, even something as simple as finding a class. Well, you're going to have to **work** for it this time...*

Difficulty: B
Current Objective: Find a dual class book
Current Rewards: 250XP, 25 silver, Dual class book
Progress: 0/3

"It's a chain quest, just like the other one," Bob said. "You'll need to complete multiple steps before the quest is done."

"Yup," the woman said. "You *might* be able to find a dual class book in the Gorm Dungeon between here and Brick Town. If you manage to complete the other two objectives, come back to me, and I'll give you the Hammerer class."

"Thank you," Keith said, inclining his head to the woman, and he *meant* it.

He'd been worried that he would need to give up on using his favorite method of fighting. Despite being good with bladed weapons, he'd always preferred using his own body as a living weapon. Fighting monsters had made that extremely difficult, but if it all worked out, he might still be able to incorporate it into his fighting style.

He was about to go, when he paused and turned back to the old woman.

"Sorry," he said, feeling a bit embarrassed. "I forgot to ask for your name."

"I'm Griss," the woman said, easily hefting the hammer onto her shoulder. "Hope your quest goes well, whelp. I'd hate to see a potential student die, seeing as I so very rarely have someone interested in my class."

"I'll do my best not to," Keith replied.

He then bowed his head once more and headed back toward the blacksmith.

"Do you know why the system seems to not like me?" he asked, remembering the odd wording of the quest. "It's been making a lot of strange comments since I came into this world."

"The creator of the system thought it would be funny to give it a personality," Bob said, rolling his eyes. "Don't mind the tone it uses. Just read the words, understand the message, and ignore the insults. That's what's important."

"Do you know who created the system?" he asked.

"Sorry," Bob replied. "That's one thing I can't tell you. Also, don't ask me why I can't tell you because I can't tell you that either."

This only made Keith more curious, but seeing as he wasn't likely to get any answers from the monkey, he decided to change the subject.

"What other hybrid items are there?" he asked. "I've already heard about hybrid armor and now a hybrid class."

"There are hybrid potions, weapons, items, and just about everything else you can think of. There are even hybrid monsters. However, all things hybrid will be more difficult and expensive to obtain. Additionally, while hybrid things offer a greater range of effects, they are weaker than the original item focused on."

"What do you mean?" Keith asked.

"Use the class you're looking for as an example," Bob said as they got into line by the blacksmith. "The hammerer class focuses on destruction and likely gives you big boosts to strength. However, whatever hybrid class you get will give you a far lesser boost to that stat while simultaneously giving you access to another boost."

"So I'll get a lesser version of each," Keith said. "That makes sense."

In his book, having more than a single trick to rely on was better than having an overwhelming advantage in one. Be super strong but have no speed, and you were basically useless. You couldn't hurt anyone if you were too slow to hit them.

"If there's such a thing as a hybrid class, can you add more than two classes together?"

"You technically can," Bob said. "But you'd need to find a tri-class book and speak with multiple class trainers. The book is so rare it's basically nonexistent, and while the bonuses are great, focusing on too many things at once is detrimental."

That much was true, Keith knew. Focus on a couple of things, and you could be fairly good at both – not as good as if you would focus on a singular thing to the exclusion of all others, but you would still come out ahead. Spread yourself too thin, and you would end up knowing nothing at all.

"You're back just in time," Sally said as they moved up to the front of the line. "If you're still interested in selling the armor you're wearing, come back after putting this on."

Keith took the set of medium scale armor, quite liking the look. He also took the small box, and when opened, saw a creepy-looking black orb hanging by a tan string – the vitality-boosting item.

"Thanks," he said, scooping the items up. "I'll be back in a bit."

He headed to his room to change this time, knowing it would be easier, despite the cold. His room was just slightly larger than the bathroom stall and would offer a bit more privacy. It didn't take long to change, and although the armor felt a bit heavier, he didn't have any problems moving with it on.

The armor looked quite impressive, the stone scales overlapping across his chest in a mesmerizing gradient from tan to black and back again. A small patch of scales covered his elbows as well, which would allow him to strike harder blows with the limb. The pants contained some scales over the shins and around the waist, while the boots were scaled on top and around the toe.

The pauldron sat on his left shoulder, sticking up a bit, and strapped across his chest. It would serve to better protect the limb, but without another to balance it, he would still be more vulnerable on the uncovered side.

Lastly, he looped the eye over his neck and found that there was a spot to tuck it in beneath the shirt, for which he was glad. He wouldn't have wanted to fight with that thing swinging around everywhere.

"How do I look?" Keith asked the monkey, who'd been sitting on the bed, watching him.

"Like a human wearing armor," Bob replied, much to his annoyance.

"You could have at least humored me," he muttered, pulling the cloak from his inventory and attaching it to the hooks at the front of the armor.

"Humoring is not my job," Bob replied, sounding very smug for some reason.

Keith simply rolled his eyes, then headed out the door. They had a quest to start, and he was determined to make good time going to that dungeon.

18

"Hey, Keith! Wait up!"

Keith paused near the exit of the guildhall, having decided to hang on to the ripper armor, just in case this pair became damaged. He paused, surprised to see Jared pushing his way through the crowd.

"Glad to see you back on your feet," Keith said, noticing the copper chain around the man's waist.

"Cayla tells me I have you to thank for that," the man said, seeming serious.

"If not for you, we might all have died," Keith replied. "What you did was extremely stupid, though. I hope you don't go making a habit of it."

"Yeah," he said, the seriousness vanishing behind a sheepish grin. "Cragg gave me a serious chewing out after he heard what I did. Still, he let me into the guild, which was all I wanted anyway."

"So what are you doing now?" he asked, deciding to steer the subject away from Jared's near-death experience.

"Going to patrol the nearby mountain pass," Jared said. "Figured I could do a scouting quest before I got back into monster hunting. It doesn't pay as well, but it's a lot safer."

"What about Cayla? Is she coming with you?"

"Nah," he replied. "She's already off on some quest with a group. She's pretty skilled for someone at her level, and when they asked her to join, she couldn't say no."

"That's good to hear," Keith said. "And speaking of, I've got a quest of my own to complete, so I'll be seeing you around."

"Yeah, definitely," Jared said, raising his hand. "If you ever need any help, just holler. I feel like after we survived something like that basher together, it's the least I can do."

"Same to you," Keith said, raising his as well. "See you around."

With that said, he turned and left, heading out of the guildhall and into the gloomy outdoors. It was colder than the day before, and a light breeze ruffled his short hair as he walked down the street, headed for the town wall. The combination of the cloak and armor did a pretty good job of keeping him warm. Additionally, since the shoulders rounded higher on this one, the cloak protected his ears from the cold, especially on the side with the pauldron.

"So," Keith said, addressing the monkey on his shoulder. "How far *is* this dungeon from here?"

"Two, maybe three days on foot," Bob replied.

"Is there anywhere we can find a horse?"

"Not in your price range," the monkey said. "Also, horses are impractical for most of this region. You'd want something nimbler and more sure-footed, like a goatpaca."

"Goatpaca?" Keith asked with a raised eyebrow.

"A mix between a mountain goat and an alpaca," Bob replied, completely serious. "The goat alone wouldn't be strong enough to carry a full-grown human."

"Why an alpaca of all things, though?" Keith asked. "Wouldn't a horse or donkey have been better?"

"*You* try mating a horse with a goat and see how that goes for you," Bob said with a laugh.

"But a goat and alpaca, two completely different animals, are no problem at all," Keith said sarcastically.

"They're compatible," replied Bob. "But I wouldn't expect you to understand, as you're not trying to become a breeder."

Keith decided to drop the topic, seeing as it didn't seem to be going anywhere, instead focusing on the reason he'd brought this up in the first place.

"If I can't get a horse, where can I find a goatpaca?"

"You'd need to go to a breeder," Bob said. "There's generally one in every settlement larger than a village, so there should be at least two in this town. However, I should warn you that they're not cheap to buy, tend to attract monsters, and require food, water, and constant care, just like any animal."

"Walking it is then," Keith said, not wanting to attract any more trouble than necessary.

It didn't take them long to reach the town wall, and once they were outside, he turned to his guide.

"Alright then, which way?"

"Through the forest, where we fought the basher last night," Bob said.

"Where *we* fought the basher?" Keith asked, heading in the indicated direction.

"I gave you vital information for defeating the monster," Bob defended. "So I would call it a team effort.

Deciding that it wouldn't be worth the effort to get into an argument, Keith chose to remain silent on the matter and just focus on the road ahead as he entered the pine forest.

"Would you mind pulling up the map so I can see where we're going?"

"I don't see why you'd need a map when you have me."

"Just humor me," Keith said. "I'd like to see what the landscape ahead looks like."

"Fine," Bob replied, sounding a little annoyed. "Here's your stupid map."

The map appeared, superimposed over his vision and forcing him to stop. He might have been annoyed, if not for the fact that he could now see where they were headed. It looked like he needed to work his way through a small section of this forest, then out into another mountain pass. From there, he would wind downward until he came to a cavern at its base, over which a small flag was pinned, connecting him to the destination.

He dismissed the map and continued walking, deciding to try asking the monkey a few questions to soothe his bruised ego.

"Why did my Monster Hunter skill immediately become upgraded to beginner from novice when I got it? I've never hunted monsters before."

"If you hunted at all, a small portion of that experience will translate over into the Monster Hunter skill," Bob replied, a tinge of annoyance still coloring his voice, but as Keith continued asking questions, that annoyance quickly began to fade.

"If that's the case, why isn't there some sort of regular hunter skill?"

"There is," Bob replied. "However, that was likely wrapped up in your Discerning Eye and Tactician skills. Monster hunting is an art of its own in this world, and because of that, got its own skill."

Keith nodded, satisfied with this answer.

"I had another question, this one about a couple of my skills," he continued. "The Bladed Mastery skill says I can wield any bladed weapon up to legendary quality without restriction. Does that mean that all higher-quality items have restrictions to using them?"

"Pretty much any item at epic or above will have restrictions attached to them due to the fact that they tend to have specialized effects. For example, an epic sword wouldn't just be a regular sword. It would give the wielder additional powers and effects, such as lightning or ice damage.

"Additionally, epic armor and above can give you set bonuses, so wearing a certain number of pieces is to your benefit. Because of this, they will all have restrictions."

"So, because of my skill, I can wield any bladed weapon up to legendary, with zero restriction?" Keith asked. "Seems a bit overpowered to me."

"Yup," Bob replied. "You could literally use the Sword of Gracious Glory or the Spear of Black Mane, despite their level, class, and stat requirements."

"I take it those are legendary weapons?" Keith asked.

"Yeah," Bob replied. "It's why I can't understand why you would willingly give up such a massive advantage and go for something different."

"Because that's exactly what he would want," Keith said, glaring up at the sky.

"Who?" Bob asked, clearly confused.

"Never mind," he replied. "Let's just say that using bladed weapons is out of the question. Maybe a thrown dagger every once in a while, but that's about it."

In his mind, the fact that the Bladed Mastery skill was so good was an obvious indicator that The Trickster wanted him to lean on it for some reason. He wasn't going to fall for it this time. Sure, he was taking a more difficult path because of it, but in the end, it would only be to his benefit.

He and Bob lapsed into silence after that, Keith focusing on running until his stamina grew too low, then slowing to a walk and waiting for it to recover before repeating the process. Now that he was in the forest and off established roads, his Ranger skill helped him move faster. By the end of the day, he had nearly reached its border.

As he'd traveled, Bob had given him some exercises to train and raise his skills, which, to his credit, worked quite well.

Skill: Discerning Eye has reached Advanced level IX

Skill: Peak Health has reached Advanced level IX

Keith laid out his bedroll below one of the towering pines, where he sat, eating dried biscuits and meat and sipping from his canteen. It wasn't the greatest he'd ever eaten, but it *was* filling, and after a long day of running, he was feeling quite hungry.

"Why am I not sore?" he asked as he tucked his canteen away.

"You didn't take any damage," Bob replied. "And while you might normally have gotten the fatigued debuff on a run like that, your skill, Peak Health, kept that from happening. It's quite a handy skill to have. Honestly, at this rate, we might reach the dungeon by tomorrow evening, especially if you keep up the same pace you did today."

"I like the sound of that," he said, getting into his bedroll.

He kept both his armor and cloak out this time, as he estimated the temperature now to be in the mid-twenties and assumed it would drop into the teens. The thick pine cover would insolate him from the wind, but he'd need to stay bundled up to remain warm through the night. A fire was out of the question, especially in a world like this one, where monsters roamed about.

Bob ducked into the sleep roll as well, curling up atop his chest, and was asleep in seconds. While it took him a bit longer, Keith – oddly enough – had no trouble falling asleep as well, *far* faster than he had in his room at the guild.

19

Just as Bob had predicted, he and Keith reached the bottom of the mountain pass by early evening the next day, where a massive opening in the stone revealed a spacious cavern within. Much to his surprise, he'd seen several people on his way over here and now found himself staring at a small building inside the cavern.

"What *is* that?" he asked, furrowing his brow.

"Probably a guild outpost," Bob said. "I'm guessing this would be one of your guild's dungeons, otherwise they wouldn't have sent you here."

"Guilds can own dungeons?" Keith asked, stepping into the cavern and noticing the temperature go up.

"Not really," Bob replied. "No one 'owns' a dungeon. They just claimed it within their territory. If anyone from another guild wants to enter, they'll be charged a toll, but anyone in *their* guild can enter for free."

True to what he'd said, Keith saw a man step out of the building as he approached the very obvious entrance to the dungeon – a stone archway intertwined with ancient-looking petrified vines.

"Hold it right there," the man said, extending a hand to stop his approach. "I don't recognize you. I'll need to inspect you, and based on what I find, will respond accordingly."

That sounds oddly ominous, Keith thought.

"Go ahead," he said with a shrug.

Once again, he got that same uncomfortable feeling that someone was analyzing him, but after a moment, it stopped and the man grew far friendlier.

"A new recruit of the guild, I take it," he said with a smile.

When Keith nodded, his grin grew wider.

"Is this your first time in a dungeon?"

Keith nodded again.

"Alright then, some simple tips to keep you alive in there. You're only level four, so I wouldn't go down to the second level once completing the first. The floor is made of several interconnected rooms and corridors, at the end of which, you'll be running into a boss.

"It'll be a tough fight alone, so I'd recommend that once you've gotten what you came for, you should leave by coming back the way you entered. I should also tell you that as a guild member, you'll have to pay a ten percent tax on all items found within the dungeon. If you wish to buy anything, rest or recover before entering, we have a few rooms available, as well as hot food."

"That's good to know," Keith said, not liking the idea of needing to pay this guild tax. "Just out of curiosity, how much would a non-guild member be charged for entering the dungeon?"

"Non-guild members pay a twenty-five percent tax on all items found, plus a five silver entrance fee."

"That seems awfully high just to enter," Keith said with a frown.

"What they find in the dungeon, more often than not, more than makes up for it," the man replied. "Now, if there isn't anything else, you may go on in."

"I'm good, thanks," Keith replied, heading toward the dungeon entrance.

"Good luck in there," the man called. "And remember, you're better off not challenging the boss."

As soon as he walked through the archway, all sound from the outside cut off. Looking back over his shoulder, Keith could still see the archway, but oddly enough, everything past it was completely blank.

"Is this normal?" he asked, looking to Bob.

"Yeah," the monkey replied. "Dungeons are a self-contained space, so nothing from the outside will interact with anything in here, including sound."

Keith turned back, examining his surroundings with a keen eye. He was currently in a stone tunnel, the walls lit by glowing white stones and the blue-gray stone covered in patches of moss. In short, it was a regular tunnel, though with the added benefit of having light provided for him. He could see the highlighted tracks of creatures all over the floor, though judging by the size, none were very large.

"What kind of monsters show up in dungeons?" he asked, starting to walk cautiously down the tunnel.

"Dungeons are different than the outside world in that you'll encounter all sorts of monsters in here. However, the monsters in dungeons greatly differ from the ones outside. Monsters in here are generated by the dungeon's core, instead of the system, so they can range from four-legged shaggy creatures to creatures from monster races, like goblins and orcs, to even undead.

"Every dungeon will have a theme and a history, so you won't be running into an undead monster and regular goblin in the same dungeon."

"If that's the case, I'm guessing regular dungeon monsters will be easier to beat than the ones we've fought so far," Keith said.

"Correct. Many dungeons do have multiple floors, with higher-level monsters appearing on the bottom. Additionally, while there's generally only a single boss at the end of the first floor, lower ones can contain multiple bosses."

"How will I know a boss when I see one?" Keith asked. "And what exactly is the difference between a boss and a regular monster?"

"It'll be very easy to spot the differences," Bob said. "Especially with your Discerning Eye skill. There are a few types of monsters, both in and out of dungeons. You may not have noticed this, as you've really only seen one type of monster in the outside world, but if you look at its name, you'll normally see it show up in a variety of colors.

"Regular monsters, like the rippers and basher we fought, will have their name appear in white lettering. A field boss, which is a type of boss that can show up randomly, will have its name in yellow. A regular boss will be red. Next are raid bosses, monsters that will take multiple teams of fighters to take down, and their names are silver.

"Section bosses typically guard entire swaths of a continent or appear at the very bottom of ten to twelve-level dungeons. Their names will be in gold and typically take several hundred fighters working in tandem to take down. Finally, there are world bosses, monsters so tough that entire guilds have been wiped out by them. Their names will appear in blue."

"What about that monster bird we saw?" Keith asked.

"That's a legendary monster," Bob replied. "They wander around and are easily recognizable, as they are labeled as such. On a strength-level, they are on par with raid or section bosses, depending on which one."

"So, what level are the five World Monsters on then?" Keith asked, already having his suspicions, as it was literally in their name.

"Obviously, they're World Bosses. However, they're a very special type of World Boss. Far from being just regular monsters with low intelligence and high power, they exhibit greater than human levels of intelligence. In short, they're smarter than the average monster, and because of that, they are a much tougher challenge.

"However, they're also unique in that they don't exceed the common level of the continent they reside in. For example, your first World Monster is only around level thirty-five. I think."

"You *think*?" Keith asked.

"Details on them are a bit hazy," Bob said with a shrug. "I can give you all the information about them, but anything more than is readily available is uncertain."

Keith let out a sigh, then decided to drop the subject. Clearly, with a quest that would decide his family's fate, he wasn't going to be getting a lot of information. Instead, he focused on the task at hand, making it through this dungeon and finding the dual class book.

The corridor suddenly opened up, and Keith found himself in an open room. Twisted roots and vines lined the floor, walls, and ceiling. Small, black-furred creatures scurried around between them.

A quick inspection showed them what they were.

Black Rat
Level: 2
HP: 25/25

"Those things look really weak," he said, feeling a bit confused.

"I *did* tell you that monsters in here tend to be weaker than the ones out there," Bob replied.

For context, the level two ripper Keith had fought to save Bob had had 140 HP, which was significantly higher than this monster's.

"Dungeons get tougher as you go, though," Bob added. "So don't expect every fight to be an easy one."

Keith nodded, then prepared himself. He quickly did a scan of the room, seeing eight of the black rats running around, all of them level two. Taking a deep breath, he charged into the room, immediately getting the rats' collective attention.

Letting out loud squeaks, they all charged directly at him, flowing over the uneven ground with ease. While a normal person might have been tripped up by the roots, Keith had no trouble at all navigating the difficult terrain, thanks to his Ranger skill.

He couldn't exactly punch the rats, so he did the only thing he could. He kicked them.

-61, Critical

Black Rat dies.

+2 XP

"That was easy," Keith said, pausing for a moment.

His momentary lapse allowed one of the rats to leap, sinking its little teeth into his leg.

-0 damage

Once again, Keith was surprised when the rat failed to do any damage at all. Then, he remembered that his new armor had a much higher rating than the last one, with a total armor of 22. That meant that if the rat did anything less than that, he would take no damage at all.

Despite not needing to use any skills to kill these monsters, Keith still used Stonestance so he could keep raising the skill. If his past experience was any indication, using a skill would increase its level.

He killed all the rats in quick succession without taking so much as a single point of damage, receiving a total of 16 XP.

Oddly enough, once all the rats were dead, a low grinding sounded, a seam in the wall opened, and a small weathered-looking chest emerged.

"Should I be looking for hidden treasure?" Keith asked as he moved to the chest.

"Yes," Bob replied. "Dungeons often have hidden pockets containing treasure. But you should also be wary of traps."

Keith nodded as he picked the lid up to reveal several bronze coins and a piece of rotted wood.

Confused, he decided to analyze it, wondering if it was just a useless piece of junk. Much to his surprise, it *was*.

"Should I keep this?" Keith asked, looking at the piece of wood.

"No point," Bob said. "We're only at the beginning of the dungeon, so we're bound to find junk like this. Let's keep moving."

Placing the twelve bronze coins he'd found in his inventory, Keith moved into the next tunnel, going deeper into the dungeon.

20

Level Up!
Congratulations! You have reached level 5. You have 5 Stat Points to allocate.

Keith swiped a hand across his forehead and let out a long breath. He looked around the room, where the bodies of four dog-sized rats were disappearing as the dungeon reabsorbed them. He'd been in here for over two hours now and had finally come across something that could hurt him.

"Congratulations," Bob said, echoing the system. "You're now the same level as an average person."

Keith just grunted in reply, slumping against the wall and letting out a low groan. He needed to take a few minutes after that last fight, as he had not been expecting them to ambush him from above.

Had he not gotten a warning just before they attacked, things might not have gone so smoothly. Now, more than ever, he was grateful for his Discerning Eye skill, which was what he likely owed his life to.

"I think I'm going to assign my points now, before we go any deeper," Keith said. "Any suggestions?"

"Well, your vitality is up a good deal, so I think we can leave that be. Your endurance could use some more, same as your strength and agility. I'd recommend putting two in agility and endurance and only one in strength this time."

Keith opened his status, then hesitated.

"Should I keep ignoring stats like wisdom and luck though?" he wondered.

He felt that having a bit more of either couldn't hurt.

"Yes, until after you get your class and see where you'll get your bonuses," Bob replied. "Then we can reassess."

"Speaking of," Keith said as he assigned the points where Bob had recommended. "Should I be trying to avoid leveling up? Won't I be missing out on extra stat points if I don't have a class?"

"You'll get any points retroactively once you get one," Bob replied. "And you'll get them as though you'd gotten the class at level one."

"I like that," Keith said. "By the way, you mentioned back when we first met Marj that he had a legendary class. How did you know, and how can I get one of those?"

"Just look a little deeper when analyzing someone," Bob said. "You always skim the information, but with your skill, you could see their entire status if you wanted. Stats, skills, skill *levels*, even what items they're wearing."

"That sounds a bit intrusive," Keith said.

"If your life is on the line, would you hesitate to find out all you can about your enemy?" Bob asked.

"No," he answered.

"Then the next time we come up against a tough-looking monster, I recommend you look a little deeper. After all, isn't knowing your enemy half the battle?"

Keith nodded in agreement. This system was taking a bit of getting used to, but every time he spoke with Bob, his knowledge increased just a bit more. He would make sure to use his skills to the utmost potential so that he could complete the quest given to him by The Trickster and go home to live a normal mortal life with his family.

"You still haven't answered my other question," he said. "How would I get a legendary class? And how much better are they than regular classes?"

"A legendary class can only be obtained through a specific item or quest," Bob replied. "Classes grow and evolve as you level. When you hit level fifteen, you'll be given the option to specialize your class, which means more bonuses in more focused areas. Every fifteen levels after that, you'll be offered another upgrade.

"Find the correct quest, and you'll have the opportunity to change a regular class to legendary. As for how they're better, let's just say you get more perks and bonuses than an average class. Now, if that's all, I really think we should keep going. We've still gotta clear this dungeon."

Keith nodded in agreement, though he took the chance to fully look over his status before closing it.

Status

Name: Keith
Race: Human
Class: None
Level: 5
XP: 8/500

HP: 120/120
MP: 0/0
STA: 160/160

Strength - 17 (16+1)
Vitality - **12** (Base 10)
Endurance - 16 (14+2)
Agility - 15 (13+2)
Intelligence - 0
Wisdom - 12
Luck - 5

Skills

Passive
Bladed Mastery: Advanced – X
Ranged Mastery: Intermediate – IV
Martial Arts: Master – V
Peak Health: Advanced – IX
Tactician: Advanced – V
Quick Learner: Advanced – V
Ranger: Advanced – III
Punisher: Master – I
Discerning Eye: Advanced – IX
Monster Hunter: Beginner – V

Active
Stonestance: Novice - IX
Brutal Rain: Novice - IV

Equipped Items

Armor
Medium Scaled Basher Shirt
Medium Scaled Basher Pants
Medium Scaled Basher Boots
Medium Scaled Basher Pauldron

Total Armor Rating: 22

Weapons
None

Other
Basher's Eye

Aside from his level, a few of his skills had grown as well. Monster Hunter, Stonestance and Brutal Rain had all gotten better. Keith was a bit disappointed that no new skills were appearing for him to learn but figured he should be grateful to have what he did thus far.

"Alright," he said, closing his status and pushing himself to his feet. "Let's keep moving."

The two of them headed into yet another tunnel after collecting the single silver coin from the chest, as well as the small lump of rusted-looking metal.

Name: Iron Ore
Crafting Material for weapons, armor, and other items
Quality: Common
Value: No less than 2 silver, 15 bronze

"The dungeon gives out ore?" Keith asked as he placed it in his inventory.

"Dungeons give out a lot of things," Bob said. "But yes, they are one of the most common places to find metal ore."

The two of them headed down the next corridor, emerging into a massive cavern, the ceiling pulling away from them. An ancient tree sat against the far wall, with a dark hole at its center. To the left and right of the tree were two archways, one presumably leading deeper into the dungeon, while the other would take them out.

The ancient tree seemed to blanket the entire room, roots twisting over the floor, leaves covering the ceiling, and vines covering the walls. In short, even without seeing the archways, Keith would have assumed this was the end of the floor.

"Looks like we've reached the boss room," Bob said, confirming his theory.

"Already?" Keith asked. "I was expecting it to be..."

"Harder to get here?" Bob said.

"Yeah," Keith replied, his brows coming down.

He'd been expecting to have to fight through at least a few more rooms before reaching this place. The last four rats he'd fought had all been level four, and although it had been a bit of a tougher battle, it hadn't been extremely difficult once he'd gotten his footing.

"I'm not surprised," Bob said, scanning the room. "You *were* sent here, which means that this floor of the dungeon must be for beginners. I-"

Bob cut off as a loud sound, something between a squeal and a roar, echoed throughout the large room, making Keith take a step back. A looming shadow appeared in the opening in the tree, and a moment later, a rat unlike anything Keith had ever seen stepped out.

It stood on two thick, muscled legs covered in pitch-black fur. The rodent stood around six feet tall and had a physique that would have made a bodybuilder green with envy.

"Are those boxing gloves?" Keith asked, seeing a barbaric version of the familiar items wrapped around the gigantic rat's paws.

"You know what I said about this being for beginners?" Bob asked as the rat crooked its thick, muscled neck from side to side.

"Yeah?" Keith asked as it fixed its small, beady eyes on him.

"Disregard everything I said," Bob said, sounding panicked. "This is not going to be an easy fight. In fact, if I were you, I'd turn around and-."

"Oh no," Keith muttered as he glanced over his shoulder to see what had brought the monkey up short.

Vines had twined over their exit, so thick that he couldn't see through to the other side.

"Forgot that could happen sometimes," Bob said with a wince. "Sorry."

"It's alright," Keith said, sizing the boss up.

Despite the way this rat looked, this fight was right in his wheelhouse. Hand-to-hand was his specialty, and while this Boss might be tough, he was sure he could out-box it if need be. Still, Keith needed to know all he could about this monster, so he focused on it using his Discerning Eye, its name immediately showing up in red letters.

Savage, Champion of the Tree
Boss Monster
Level: 9
Class: Brute Boxer
HP: 1,800/1,800
STA: 1,950/1,950

Str - 42
Agi - 37
Lck - 10

Skills: (P) Champion, Boxing, Fleetfoot, Wall (A) Fourfold Combo, Power Cross, Bloody Uppercut, Savage Unleashed (AOE)

"Why is it just standing there?" Keith asked after doing a quick scan.

"It won't attack until you are fully in the room," Bob replied. "Dungeons are designed this way to give people a chance to prepare. Otherwise, no one would make it out of a boss room alive."

"Well, if that's the case," Keith said, then delved deeper into the monster's status.

Apparently, the reason only its strength, agility, and luck scores showed up was because its vitality and endurance were obvious by how much health and stamina it had. Both were staggering to see.

Apparently, boss monsters had a good deal more stopping power than the average, as his own health pool was a pathetic one-twenty when compared to the monster's absolutely massive 1,800. And that was not to mention the fact that it was nearly twice his current level.

"How is an ordinary person expected to take something like this on?" Keith asked as he finished examining each of the monster's skills in detail.

"They're *not*," Bob said. "Normal people would tackle a dungeon in a team of three to five. You're a freak of nature, though, so you'll likely be able to deal enough damage to beat it on your own. *If* you manage not to get hit."

"Great," Keith said, dragging the cloak off his shoulders and loosening up. "Let's see if I can trash this rat."

"Good luck with that," Bob said. "I'll be hiding while you do that. Don't die. Please."

With that said, the monkey ditched him to fight the monster rat on his own.

21

Keith was quite confident in defeating the overgrown rodent, but he had to be wary of its skills and higher strength and agility. With those, it would be faster and hit much harder than he could, so he'd need to rely on his skills to tell him where the rat would be and predict its movements.

One of his many martial arts instructors over the years had likened a fight to a game of chess. One had to constantly be thinking several moves ahead if they wanted to prevail. In this fight, a single mistake could cost him his life.

Keith let out a long breath, then stepped fully into the room, approaching the massive rat that had – until now – remained eerily still. As soon as he moved, the rat became animated once more, its snout bunching up in a snarl and revealing a nasty row of needle-like teeth.

However, much to his surprise, the monster didn't immediately charge him, instead raising both of its hands and waiting for him to approach. This told Keith that the rat would be approaching this fight like an official match instead of a brawl.

Good to know, he thought, mimicking the rat's posture and slowly circling to its left.

The rat slowly turned, keeping its stance steady and its eyes locked on him. Keith tried circling to the left, only for the rat to do the same. It seemed that this monster was well-trained.

Okay, he thought. *Let's see how it handles a real fighter.*

Keith moved in, his motions smooth and practiced. Several spots stood out on the rat's body – areas in which its guard was down and left openings to strike. This was a bit different than the weak spots on the monster's body, as those stood out in purple and were behind the rat's guard.

The openings were being shown in red to differentiate between the two. For example, the rat's center – where he would strike to knock the wind out of it – was glowing purple. However, with the way the rat was holding its arms, that area was well-protected.

On the other hand, the rat's thighs and shins were outlined in red, showing an opening to strike. If this monster fought like a classic boxer, it meant all he really needed to watch out for were its fists. However, as one of his many teachers had once told him, 'you don't chop a tree down at the top.'

When the rat telegraphed a punch at his head, Keith was already ducking beneath, his leg sweeping out in a shortened roundhouse kick and slamming into the side of the monster's leg.

-18

The rat let out an angry shriek, then tried to back off to get a good punch, only for Keith to stick close and low. Another punch swished by overhead, and Keith stepped around to kick the other leg.

-18

Instead of stepping back this time, the rat stepped forward, driving a punch down to try catching him off-guard, but with Keith's tactician skill and master level Martial Arts skill, he saw the attack coming from a mile away. As the rat stepped forward, he stepped to the side. When it punched down, he struck its exposed ribs, triggering his Brutal Rain as he did.

-34

-32

He stepped around after the second punch, following the rat's only possible course of action. After all, if he had been struck in the ribs and had been limited to the fighting style of a boxer, he'd have turned to try punching as well.

In short, he followed the monster's movement, then struck the same exposed spot twice more.

-34

-38

The crackling blue light of Brutal Rain vanished after the fourth blow once more. Although the skill didn't have a set number of attacks, Keith was now under the assumption that the maximum would be four. Perhaps that number would go up when he hit the Beginner ranks, but he would cross that bridge when he got there.

The rat let out another squealing roar, then feigned another punch, only to step back, trying once again to put some distance between them.

Keith allowed the rat to do so. Fights like these were about strategy as much as actual power. He had far less stamina than this monster, so he needed to take the time to recover between exchanges.

He'd noticed that his last attack had done more damage than the first three, and the spot of purple on the rat's ribs had grown noticeably darker. It seemed that repeatedly striking the same area over and over again would weaken it, just as he'd suspected.

At this point, after having failed to actually land any attacks, the rat would likely lean on one of its skills to try hitting him. Its pride as a fighter would be stinging right about now, and that might make it careless. If he had to guess, it would either use its Power Cross – a skill that both increased strength *and* speed of its cross punch – or Bloody Uppercut, which added to the damage in the actual gloves.

If the monster was close, Keith thought it would use the latter. It had created distance, so the former was more likely. In other words, he'd need to watch out for the cross and ignore the rest.

The rat shuffled in once more, and Keith focused. This rat was far faster than he currently was. The only way he was managing to stay in this fight was due to his own skill and experience.

With a squeal, the rat launched into a wild hook, the spiked boxing glove on a collision course with the side of his head. Keith was already dodging back, his leg sweeping up and slamming into its open side.

-18

However, he hadn't accounted for the rat's weight. Had this been a normal fighter, this would have thrown them back a few steps, but with his current strength stat, it apparently wasn't enough.

Keith stumbled back instead of the rat, putting him off-balance, and the boss took advantage of his mistake. It charged in, dropping its guard and unleashing a barrage of vicious hooks and crosses, forcing Keith to desperately retreat.

It was a case where his own training and experience had worked against him. Even a larger person would have been knocked back, but that rat had to weigh some fifteen-hundred pounds, at the very least. It was a simple mistake, one drilled into him over countless hours, and now, it had put him on the back foot.

He almost missed it when the skill was activated, but thankfully, he was still able to keep his wits about him.

The rat struck forward, and its entire arm was surrounded by a red glow. Keith dropped to his stomach, the Power Cross managing to graze the top of his head, despite his quick reaction.

-16 damage

Keith spun his body, kicking around the monster as it punched down, the glowing glove slamming into the floor and sending chips of wood spinning into the air. He was lucky this rat seemed to abide by the principles of its fighting style. Had it not, it would have kicked him square in the ribs instead of trying to punch him.

The boss turned, trying to predict where he'd land, and punched once more. Keith barely avoided being hit by rolling onto his back. He saw the opening the instant he did, and with his centuries of experience, capitalized on it in an instant.

He used Stonestance, even as he struck upward with both legs, his hands placed behind his head for maximum force. Both feet caught the rat – now off-balance, thanks to its hunched position – square in its chest.

-8

The damage was negligible, as he hit a well-muscled area, which he assumed acted like armor, but this time, the rat's weight worked against it. With a loud squeal, it stumbled back, arms flailing as it tried to maintain its balance. Keith sprang back to his feet and immediately brought his knee up into the Boss' face as its upper body forward, rebalancing after its near-fall in the opposite direction.

It was the perfect shot, and had this been another world, Keith likely would have killed his opponent with this maneuver. However, this wasn't another world, so the boss didn't immediately die. Still, the damage was impressive, to say the least.

-220, Massive Critical

Savage is stunned for 5 seconds.

Keith pounced on the monster, unleashing several hammerfists to its temple as it lay there, frozen like a statue. Helpless to defend itself, the boss took several heavy hits before the stun wore off, but by then, Keith had managed to whittle its HP down to half.

He quickly moved back, a second before the stun wore off. It wouldn't do to be greedy and get caught in the process.

With a roar, Savage burst back into motion, a fist flashing up and swiping through the area where he'd been standing a second ago. Keith waited for the monster to stand, eyeing his stamina.

He currently had about a third remaining. Keith reached into his inventory for a potion. Savage faced him, blood running down the side of its face, as Keith downed the yellow potion, his stamina bar climbing by fifty points.

The rat's face was scrunched up in obvious rage. If looks could kill, Keith would be a smoking corpse, he was sure. Still, as far as he knew, this rat could only kill him if it made physical contact.

The rat's muscles flexed, its body glowed crimson, and Keith knew he would be dodging for his life. It seemed the rat was finally going to stop holding back and go on an all-out offensive, which it should have done since the start.

It had higher health and stamina, so it could afford to be wasteful. Its opponent, on the other hand, could not.

"Well, poop," Keith muttered.

He'd been hoping the boss wouldn't realize this for a while yet. Now that it had, Keith's chances of survival went way down. A single grazing blow had shaved off sixteen points of his health. He could hardly imagine what an actual full-on attack would do.

22

Savage moved forward blindingly fast, and it was only thanks to his skill that Keith managed to avoid taking it full-on. Still, the glowing fist managed to clip his shoulder, spinning him around and almost knocking him off his feet.

-4 damage

Keith reoriented, instinctively dropping in a squat and avoiding the powerful sweeping hook meant to knock his head from his body. He stood, stepping quickly to his left and avoiding yet another punch but didn't manage to land an attack before the rat stepped back, then drove forward.

It was currently using its Fourfold Combo skill, one that would elevate its power, speed, and accuracy, so long as it only used four punches in a specific order. This skill could go on for as long as the boss had stamina to burn, and with a truly massive pool, it could keep going for a while.

However, that grazing punch had told him something important. Just as the monsters had weak points, so did he. Keith had been so focused on his opponent's that he'd failed to examine his. The last two attacks he'd taken had opened his eyes.

A punch to his unarmored head had done sixteen points of damage, while a punch to his heavily armored left shoulder had done almost nothing. If he had to take a blow, he would need to make sure he took it in a way that did the least amount of damage – just like in any fight.

The boss kept advancing, its blazing red body moving quickly and in a smooth, endless combination of punches, backing Keith around the room. He had to be careful, as the footing was uneven, and he was reacting. The boss's punches were only growing faster, and while before he was barely managing to stay ahead, now he was only surviving by the skin of his teeth.

"You might wanna hit back!" Bob's voice echoed from somewhere in the cavern, causing Keith to flinch.

This cost him as the boss's glowing fist smacked into the side of his ribs, tossing him back half a step.

-40 damage

Keith gritted his teeth against the pain that radiated through his side. The armor there wasn't exactly thick, but it *was* thick enough to offer some protection. His HP was slowly ticking back up, but his stamina kept dropping. He needed to create an opening so he could take a few potions, but the rat wasn't going to be giving him that time so easily.

He dodged right, then left. He ducked and weaved, barely managing to stay alive as the rat continued throwing punch after punch. Its stamina had dipped to about half, and although Keith wasn't keeping exact time, he estimated around forty seconds before it ran dry.

Which means it will have to drop the skill soon, he thought, feeling a small spark of hope kindle in his chest.

He just had to last until then.

The blazing red fists continued coming, the air around them seeming to hum every time it struck. Keith managed to avoid about a dozen more before he was just a hair too slow avoiding a jab. He winced as a line of burning pain traced its way across his cheek, and a damage notification flashed before his eyes.

-22 damage

One of the spikes on the glove had cut him as it had passed, but thankfully, he didn't get slapped with a bleeding debuff. It seemed he'd need to take a far more severe hit to be saddled with one of those.

Still, another hit meant more health lost. A quick glance told him he had about half left. Keith's stamina, on the other hand, was dangerously low.

He was breathing harder, sweat beading on his brow as he continued to avoid the monstrous rat. The boss's stamina dropped to forty percent, as his dropped to 10/160. Desperation started to claw at the back of his mind, begging him to try to make an opening, but he knew this would be a mistake.

The rat *was* leaving plenty of openings, but if he were foolish enough to try taking one of them, he would end up dead before he could so much as blink. No, his only hope was to keep dodging and pray the rat would stop to preserve its stamina.

Savage continued punching, and Keith continued dodging.

Jab, cross, hook, uppercut. Jab, cross, hook, uppercut. Jab, hook, jab, cross.

The punches continued coming in rapid succession, the monster changing up the combinations every few seconds to try catching him off guard. Its unpredictability was what made it predictable, as the monster could only use four punches.

If it continuously used the exact same order each and every time, Keith might think it was plotting, trying to lure him into a false sense of security right before throwing a hook instead of a cross. This was honestly the only reason he was still alive, because despite the changes in the combination, the monster could only use those four punches, so long as this skill was active.

His stamina dropped to 4/160, as the boss's hit 35% and finally, the red glow around the monster vanished.

Keith immediately leaped back, pulling a stamina potion from his inventory and downing it in a single gulp. The monster charged in again, throwing an overhead cross and stopping him from grabbing his final potion.

Still, even as he avoided this punch, Keith felt his panic recede. He couldn't afford to use any active skills at the moment, but he could now resume his attack on the monster.

Savage stumbled past as he overshot an attack, and Keith's fist came up, hammering the monster in its ribs.

-32

Unfortunately, he couldn't aim well with the monster moving as it was and was unable to get a good shot at the same spot. However, as the monster whirled, predictably trying to backhand him, he stepped back, then forward as the fist passed.

His body twisted as his leg drove forward, slamming into the monster's exposed knee. The spot had flared a bright purple the instant before the rat had attacked and was now glowing even brighter.

While the front of the knee was a difficult spot to hit – not to mention ineffective – the side or back of the knee would cause a good deal of damage.

-80, Critical

Savage is crippled.

-25% Agility

The monster squealed, dropping to one knee and leaving Keith with the perfect target. His body twisted and his other leg came up in a sweeping blow, smashing into the monster directly between the legs.

However, instead of the massive critical he'd been expecting, Keith felt his foot come up against some resistance.

-16

Savage is Enraged. That was a low blow. Too bad it didn't work this time.

"A *cup*?" he exclaimed, genuinely shocked for the first time since the battle had started.

All Martial Artists would generally wear something to protect their private areas while fighting. However, the last thing he'd expected was that this rat would do the same.

The rat's eyes rolled back into its head and its veins stood out all along its body. Keith quickly stumbled back as it unleashed a roar of rage, his vision going a bit fuzzy.

You are intimidated: -50% focus for 3 seconds.

He shook his head, trying to clear the fog, but it refused to go. On instinct, he ducked, pulling his hands up to guard his face. He felt a hard impact and staggered back as a damage notification flashed in his mind's eye – somehow perfectly clearly.

-55 damage

You are stunned for 3 seconds.

His muscles locked up as his vision cleared. The rat towered over him, looking like a demon out of a nightmare. Its body was practically steaming, and with its eyes rolled back into its head, it looked to be completely unhinged.

His HP was near zero, and he was frozen for the next couple of seconds. It would appear that this was the end – again. Then the unexpected happened, as a small, multicolored shape blurred down from the ceiling, landing on the rat's face and covering its eyes.

Keith only had a moment to be completely shocked once more before Bob leaped off the rat's face, latching onto a vine and hauling himself up into the cover of the tree, where he sat, trembling from head to toe.

Thankfully, that simple distraction had bought Keith the time he needed. Finally able to move again, he pulled two healing potions from his inventory, downing them one after the next, as the enraged rat tried to jump and catch the out-of-reach monkey.

Next, Keith removed his last stamina potion, downing that as well. Finally, he removed his armor potion, though he didn't immediately drink it, tucking it into a safe and easy-to-reach spot in his armor.

Savage continued jumping, trying to reach the monkey, which meant that its enraged status was probably messing with its common sense.

Keith crooked his neck from side to side, then used Brutal Rain. His body surrounded by a crackling nimbus of blue energy and churning with power, he threw himself forward.

Four blows slammed into the rat's solar plexus in rapid succession, dealing a nice amount of damage and bringing it down into the yellow.

-196, Massive Critical

-172, Massive Critical

-188, Massive Critical

-202, Massive Critical

Savage is stunned for 5 seconds.

Once more, Keith pounced on the monster, bringing several hammer fists down on its temple, dropping his health into the red. However, he didn't quite manage to finish it off before the monster recovered. He would have continued attacking, but a single glance at the rat's eyes convinced him to back off.

He stood where he was, hands raised, as the monster slowly got to its feet, favoring its injured knee. The eyes were no longer rolled up into its head, which was what had caused him to back off. With the enraged status gone, the monster would be a more effective fighter, and with its HP so low, Keith had a pretty good feeling about what would be coming next.

Savage crossed both its arms, its body beginning to emit steam at a rapid rate. Slowly, the ground around him began to ripple as a crackling power began coursing across the monster's body. This was its AOE – area of effect – skill, Savage Unleashed.

The monster's strength and speed would double, and every punch would unleash a wave of power that would affect a wide area, meaning it could hit multiple targets at once and at a distance. For a boxer, it was a pretty good skill.

Hand-to-hand fighters very rarely had ranged attacks, seeing as they used no weapons. This would have been a problem for him had he not already slowed the monster down and prepared a strategy for just such a scenario.

Savage pulled his fist back, and instead of trying to run or avoid it, Keith charged directly at him, pulling the Armor potion from his belt.

A massive, spiked boxing glove made of crackling red light shot from the monster's fist as it punched, quickly expanding to cover an area roughly ten feet across. The monster immediately punched twice more, to Keith's left and right, removing any chance of him being able to avoid it.

Keith continued running, while he pulled the cork from the armor potion and downed it. In the same instant, he used his Stonestance, further adding to his defensive strength. He angled his shoulder forward, then tucked his chin. The skill slammed into him, and thanks to all of his preparations, the damage was greatly reduced.

-26 damage

Still, the fact that he took this much damage told him just how bad it would have been had he not taken the potion or used the skill. Thanks to the skill being somewhat insubstantial, Keith was able to push through it while only stumbling a bit.

Savage, seeing his approach, threw another attack, shaving off another twenty-six HP, followed by another. However, by the time the third attack came, Keith was right in his face. Savage's arm was cocked back, prepared to throw a fourth punch, when Keith's hand, shaped into a blade, struck his throat.

-192, Massive Critical

Savage is stunned for 3 seconds.

The rat staggered back, clutching at its throat and wheezing as blood leaked from its open mouth, giving Keith the opportunity to land the finishing blow. He drove his elbow forward, cracking the monster right in the eye and tossing it clean off its feet.

23

-106, Critical

Savage, Champion of the Tree, dies.

+750 XP

Level Up!
Congratulations! You have reached level 6. You have 5 Stat Points to allocate.

Skill: Monster Hunter has reached Beginner level VI

Skill: Brutal Rain has reached Novice level VI

*Skill: **Stonestance** has advanced to Beginner.*

Stonestance
Level: Beginner - I
Your body becomes as tough as stone
Cost: 20 STA
Damage: 10-16
Armor: +20%
Duration: 10 Seconds

*New active skill available: **Ghost Flash***

Ghost Flash
Project your inner power outward
Cost: 50 STA
Damage: 8-14
Additional Effects: 15% Chance to paralyze

Would you like to learn this skill? Yes/No

"Now *that's* what I'm talking about," Keith said, mentally selecting *yes* and raising a tired fist in the air as a sign of victory.

"Good job keeping yourself alive," Bob said, dropping from the ceiling and landing on his shoulder.

"You actually came to help me," Keith said, turning his head to examine the monkey out of the corner of his eye.

"Like I mentioned, if you die, I die," Bob replied. "I was only doing it out of self-preservation."

"I thought you said you couldn't fight?"

"I didn't fight," Bob said. "I just landed on the monster's face, then ran away."

Keith's lips quirked up into a smile at that. It seemed that despite being a coward, the monkey cared enough to help despite what he'd just said. He opened his mouth to say something but was momentarily distracted when a chest, shining a bright silver, rose up in front of the tree, even as the monster's corpse slowly vanished.

"Go check it out," Bob said, sounding oddly excited.

Keith didn't need to be told twice, immediately moving over to the chest and examining the contents within.

He saw several vials that glowed green, yellow, and amber. There were also a couple of lumps of metal, a small bar of gold, and a weathered-looking tome.

"Holy poop on a stick!" Keith exclaimed.

"I am unfamiliar with this saying," Bob said, sounding puzzled.

"My parents never liked when we swore," Keith explained, reaching into the chest and snagging the potions, "so I do my best not to. Needed to come up with something to use, so I settled on this."

"You're a real weirdo, you know that?" Bob said.

"Yup," Keith replied as he analyzed the potions.

Name: Middling Healing Potion (X2)
Quality: Common
Effect: Restores 100 HP
Value: 4 Silver, 50 Bronze

Name: Middling stamina Potion (X3)
Quality: Common

Effect: Restores 100 STA
Value: 4 Silver, 50 Bronze

Name: Weak Armor Potion (X3)
Quality: Uncommon
Effect: +25 Armor for 30 seconds
Value: 2 Silver, 10 Bronze

"Not bad at all," Keith said, storing all of the potions in his inventory.

These healing and stamina potions were better than the ones he'd had before, though the armor potions were worse. However, he got three of them, so he wasn't about to complain.

"Is this...?" he asked, raising the surprisingly heavy bar of gold.

"A small gold bar?" Bob said. "Yes, that is indeed a small gold bar."

Keith grinned, storing it in his inventory as well. Next, he reached in for the two lumps of metal, though one was noticeably shinier than the other. The less shiny was another piece of iron ore, but the other, he needed to check out.

Name: Nickel Ore
Crafting material for weapons, armor, and other items
Quality: Uncommon
Value: No less than 22 Silver, 88 Bronze

Keith stored that in his inventory as well, finally reaching for the last item.

Name: Dual Class Book
A book that can record a total of 2 classes and combine them into one
Quality: Rare
Value: No less than 3 small gold, 86 silver

Keith's eyes went wide. This book was even more valuable than the basher thumper.

"Does this book always drop upon defeating the boss?" he asked excitedly.

"No," Bob replied. "The only guaranteed way for this to drop is if it's a quest reward, and seeing as you only get to have one class, no one can get a quest for an item like this more than once. Unless someone pays you to retrieve it for them, in which case, you still won't get to keep it. Speaking of quests," the monkey continued. "Yours should be updating any second now."

As though on cue, a small *ping* sounded in his mind and a new message appeared.

*Quest update: **The Road Less Traveled***
*You seem to like making things difficult, even something as simple as finding a class. Well, you're going to have to **work** for it this time...*
Difficulty: B
Current Objective: Reach Brick Town and find an appropriate class teacher
Current Rewards: 150 XP, 10 silver, Desired class
Progress: 1/3

As soon as the message vanished, a couple more messages flashed across his vision.

+250 XP

You have received 25 Silver.

"It seems to me that I'm getting an absurd amount of experience for this one part of the quest," Keith said, dismissing the notification.

"Well, it seems to me that you just soloed a boss four levels higher than you and lived," Bob said. "I'd take the XP and not complain."

"Is it just me, or does it also seem like I just barely manage to avoid dying every time I get into a fight?"

"No, it's definitely not just you," Bob said. "If you picked on monsters your own level, maybe you wouldn't be in danger of dying all the time."

Keith put the dual class book in his inventory, then pulled up his status. During the last fight, he had once again come dangerously close to running out of stamina. It would be overkill to put all his available stat points into the one stat, so he put four into endurance – bringing his total stamina up to two-hundred – and put the last into strength, then took a moment to look it over.

<u>Status</u>
Name: Keith
Race: Human
Class: None
Level: 6
XP: 508/600

HP: 120/120
MP: 0/0
STA: 200/200

Strength - 18 (17+1)
Vitality - **12** (Base 10)
Endurance - 20 (16+4)
Agility - 15
Intelligence - 0
Wisdom - 12
Luck - 5

<u>Skills</u>

<u>Passive</u>
Bladed Mastery: Advanced – X
Ranged Mastery: Intermediate – IV
Martial Arts: Master – V
Peak Health: Advanced – IX
Tactician: Advanced – V
Quick Learner: Advanced – V
Ranger: Advanced – III
Punisher: Master – I
Discerning Eye: Advanced – IX
Monster Hunter: Beginner – VI

Active
Stonestance: Beginner - I
Brutal Rain: Novice - VI
Ghost Flash: Novice - I

Equipped Items

Armor
Medium Scaled Basher Shirt
Medium Scaled Basher Pants
Medium Scaled Basher Boots
Medium Scaled Basher Pauldron

Total Armor Rating: 22

Weapons
None

Other
Basher's Eye

"So," Keith said, stretching his arms over his head. "I say we go get some sleep. It's probably quite late by now. Then we'll head out early in the morning to Brick Town."

"Yeah, that sounds good," Bob said as he headed for the exit. "You've probably forgotten this in the euphoria of getting all those items, but you do realize you're going to have to pay ten percent on everything you got here, right? If my math is right, that means you'll be paying a total of around fifty-four silver."

Keith came up short, his hand moving up to clutch at his chest, and almost had a heart attack right then and there.

24

Keith and Bob headed out early the next morning, leaving the warmth of the guild outpost for the cold of the mountain pass. True to Bob's calculations, Keith had had to pay a whopping fifty-four silver coins upon exiting the dungeon, effectively wiping out half the gold bar he'd found. This left him with a grand total of seventy-eight silver and ninety-six bronze to his name.

At least he'd gotten a meal and a warm bed out of it, though judging by the smug look on that guild guard's face, he was definitely skimming off the top.

"When I make it past level fifteen, I'm going to go back and kick his scrawny behind," Keith muttered as he hiked up through the mountain pass.

"Whatever helps you sleep at night," Bob said, patting his shoulder. "Now, if you want to reach Brick Town before it gets dark, I suggest you get a move on."

Unlike on his trip here from Oster's Keep, Brick Town was close enough to the dungeon that Keith could make it there in a day if he hurried. If not, he'd be shut out of the town, forced to sleep in the freezing cold until morning, when the gates would be opened once more.

"I don't know much about how these things work," Keith said, voicing something that had been bothering him. "But aside from the XP, are the items I'm getting better than average?"

"Yup," Bob replied. "Generally, people in your position fight in parties of three to five, like you did on your quest to join the guild. Since you've been fighting mostly on your own, the system is giving you a greater reward, as the difficulty is higher. As for the quest with the basher, the reason why you got more is simple. The other two gave you their share of the loot."

A gust of wind buffeted them as they crested a ridge in the pass, and the sides of the mountain fell away to reveal a wide-open plane, stretching for several miles in all directions. Surrounding them on all sides, Keith could see more mountains, meaning that he wasn't out of the mountainous region just yet.

"How far is the nearest city from here?" he asked as they headed down to the open plain.

"Umber City is around a week and a half by foot at your current speed," Bob replied. "But I wouldn't recommend going there until you're at least level ten. While you'll have more options as far as items, shops, and countless other things, there are some shifty types there who would see you as a potential target."

"I'll wait until level ten then," Keith agreed.

He could afford to wait to go to the city. There was likely plenty for him to do around Oster's Keep anyway. And who knew? He might even pick up another quest or two in Brick Town.

The wind got worse throughout the day, sending his cloak flapping in the wind. With nothing to break against in the plains, he got the full brunt of it. Despite the effects of his cloak keeping him from getting any debuffs, Keith was quite cold by the time they reentered the mountain pass in the late afternoon.

"This place looks a lot more alive," Keith commented as he noted the numerous trees – all of them pines – flanking the sides of the path and moving higher into the mountain.

Additionally, there was brittle, dried grass everywhere, as well as signs of a source of fresh water nearby.

"Yeah," Bob replied. "Oster's Keep is far better situated for those wanting to live peacefully without the need to worry about monster attacks. Those martial artist types really seem to prefer it that way."

Keith nodded in agreement. In the previous world he'd inhabited, it wasn't uncommon for temples dedicated to the martial arts to set themselves high in the mountains, where they would be free of war and strife. Of course, that didn't help them when warlords came, trying to conscript the skilled fighters into their wars.

Many a temple had been destroyed that way – all its inhabitants butchered – with a spare few escaping to spread stories of the horrors they'd witnessed. Keith really hoped this wasn't one of *those* types of temples.

His hopes were soon dashed as the pass forked, one winding deeper into the mountains, while the other took a very steep upward slope.

"Up we go," Bob said, pointing to the sloping path.

"Great," Keith muttered, already dreading what was to come.

It took several hours more of arduous, steep climbing to reach the summit of the mountain. Several times, he'd been forced to take breaks and allow his stamina to recover. Only once Keith got to a higher peak did he finally get a good look at Brick Town. It was exactly as he'd expected it would be.

The temple was ostentatiously perched atop the highest peak, set behind and above the town. The wooden structure sat beside a cascading waterfall, one that fell thousands of feet, disappearing in a spray of mist below.

"I really hope they don't give me some stupid spiritual quest to get the class I want," he groaned as he continued down the path toward the gate.

Keith had dealt with the spiritual types before, and while a lot of them were the real deal, he had never been one to sit on a mountaintop and meditate for weeks on end, thinking about the mysteries of the universe and the true meaning of life. He had become too cynical for that during his lives on many worlds. If there was some mystical secret, it was that life wasn't fair and that if you had it good, you should keep your trap shut and enjoy it while it lasted.

Keith had frequently complained about his lot in his life with his siblings. Now, he would do literally anything to be able to see them again.

Just a little longer, he told himself, hunching his shoulders against the growing chill as he approached the gate. *Just a little longer, and you'll be able to see them all again.*

"Halt! What business do you have in Brick Town?"

A fresh-faced guard stepped forward, extending a hand clad in an iron glove and halting Keith in his tracks. The iron gloves were the only part of the guard's outfit that was metal, the rest made up entirely of cloth that looked far too thin to be worn in a climate this cold.

However, judging by the cut of the robes – the long flowing style that seemed to be favored by the mystical types – this man was a martial artist.

"I'm here looking for a class trainer," Keith replied evenly, not wishing to get on this man's bad side.

"Then you are in the wrong place, monster hunter," the man said with a sneer. "Your kind is better off on the bottom of the mountain, rolling around in the filth with your beasts."

So that's how it's going to be, Keith thought with a sigh.

This was a B-rated quest, after all, which meant no part of it could be easy.

"Look," Keith said, trying to keep his annoyance from showing. "I've had a long journey here. It's getting colder, and it'll be night soon. I'm not asking you to personally escort me to a class trainer, but could you at least let me into town?"

"That depends," the man said, eyeing him up and down.

"On?"

"On whether you can afford to pay the entry fee. The Heavenly Temple could always use contributions from willing believers."

So he wants a bribe. Typical.

These people were all mystical and universe – until *money* came up. Then they were just as greedy as everyone else.

"Will a silver coin satisfy the needs of the temple?" Keith asked, still fighting to keep his annoyance from showing.

"You can take that pathetic offering back to your rat-infested pig pen," the man snapped, looking offended.

Keith next removed five silver coins, already silently promising to get them back upon his exit. Once more though, the man turned his nose up at them. Only when he offered ten did the man seem amenable.

"The Temple thanks you for your contribution," the man said, taking his coins and pocketing them.

He then proceeded to raise his arms, taking on a threatening stance.

"Now, you'd best be on your way, filth, before you anger me."

"Please don't tell me all martial artists in this world act this way," Keith said, turning to Bob, who had, thus far, remained silent.

"Beats me," Bob said with a shrug. "I honestly didn't think these types would be so snooty."

"Maybe I should go and find a different class trainer."

"The next closest place would be Umber City," Bob replied. "The trainers there will be more expensive and not as good. I suggest you try at least getting into the town. If the rest of them are this unbearable, we can leave."

Keith turned back to the man, who was still glaring at him.

"Listen," Keith said, trying to sound reasonable.

"No," the man said defiantly. "You are trespassing on sacred ground. Now leave, or I will make you!"

Keith's eyes narrowed at that, but before he did anything, he did a quick inspection of the man.

Name: Gavin
Race: Human
Class: Iron Monk
Level: 9

Keith was interested to see that when he read a bit further, a guild name popped up.

Affiliations: Heavenly Temple Guild, Naya - Spirit of Light

"No gods in this world?" Keith asked, surprised.

"Nah," Bob replied. "The system is an egomaniac and doesn't want anyone to think there are any beings with more power than it. So, all-powerful beings that people here worship are called spirits."

"I've warned you, heathen," snapped Gavin. "Prepare to meet your end!"

It appeared that Keith had gone from regular old filth to a full-blown heathen.

"Well, that escalated quickly," Bob said as the man charged them.

"I'm not too worried," Keith replied, not even bothering to raise his hands.

While the man was higher-leveled and had a class, his primary fighting skill – Heavenly Light – was in the beginner levels. Additionally, the man's movements were clunky at best, not at all like the smooth, refined movements of a master in the martial arts.

Gavin charged in, taking a wild swing at his head, and Keith easily swayed back, avoiding the blow. Right now, he had a problem. He needed to get into the town. If he attacked this man, his chances of learning at his guild probably wouldn't be too great. Keith needed to figure out how to make this man realize that this would be a futile fight without hurting him.

"Stand still!" Gavin screamed, cocking an arm back and throwing a horribly telegraphed punch that Keith easily avoided.

It was when the man stumbled past, trying to regain his balance, that Keith noticed his stamina bar dip. He flashed back to his own experience running out of stamina, remembering well how long it had taken him to recover.

He began paying attention then, as Gavin continued to lunge and grab, trying to hit the infuriating man who just refused to go down. After about half a minute, Keith thought he had a pretty good grasp on the man's usage and regeneration rate.

With a total of two hundred, and using between twelve and fifteen every time he missed an attack and needed to correct himself, Gavin would run out within the next couple of minutes. It would then take roughly seven and a half minutes for it to fully recover before he would be able to get up and come after Keith, by which time he'd have scaled the short wall and made it up to the temple.

"Heathen!" Gavin panted, swinging again. "Stand still and accept your rightfully deserved punishment!"

"What's he going on about?" Keith asked Bob as the man once again missed.

"I don't know," the monkey replied with a shrug. "But you've gotta admit, he *is* a determined one."

Bob wasn't lying. A normal person would have seen that they had no hope of winning by this point and given up. Now, this *was* partially due to Keith barely avoiding some of his attacks to keep him thinking he could win, but still, by the time Gavin's stamina was in the red, he *should* have stopped. Instead, the dimwitted guard just kept on coming.

"Hea...then!" Gavin heaved, his breaths coming in ragged gasps. "You...will...*pay*!"

The man charged, but this time, Keith just stood still. Gavin swung, letting out a cry of victory as though he had finally succeeded, only to fall flat on his face as he ran out of stamina, the top of his head brushing against the tip of Keith's shoes as he fell.

"I'll be taking that," Keith said, stooping to collect the silver coins that had fallen from the man's pocket.

"You swine!" Gavin yelled from his prone position, unable to move. "No honorable fighter would stoop so low."

"I hate to tell you this, kid," Keith said. "Honor is for chumps. A *real* fighter will do whatever it takes to win, and fighting dirty is a term used by weaklings who can't win without significant handicaps."

He rose, clutching the handful of silver coins and placing them in his inventory.

"Coward," Gavin yelled. "I'll kill you for this!"

The threat would have sounded far more menacing had he not been lying with his nose smushed into the ground.

"You'll kill me for what?" Keith asked, sounding very innocent. "I didn't do anything. You ran out of stamina all on your own. I didn't even touch you."

Gavin opened his mouth, clearly ready to snap back, only to realize that Keith was right. He hadn't done anything. Even now, when he was lying defenseless, Keith had done nothing. Well, other than taking the coins Gavin had tricked him into giving.

If Keith had expected that knowledge to make the man feel grateful, he'd have been very disappointed. Good thing he hadn't.

"You swine! You dirty, low-down rotten piece of..."

Whatever else the man had to say was lost to him as Keith took a running leap, placed his foot into a crack in the wall, and threw himself higher. His fingers easily curled around the top, and with a flex of his arms, Keith hauled himself up to peer over the wall.

He took a moment to make sure no one would see him before pulling himself up and over, hitting the ground and tucking into a roll before coming up to his feet.

"Well," Keith said, dusting off his armor. "That was easy enough."

25

The town itself wasn't really much to look at. A single main street stretched before him, splitting the town in two. Several houses and smaller shops lined the street – Keith counted about fourteen per side – where several people moved about.

To his right and left, he saw two more streets, showing another row of buildings to either side, but that was it. The entire town was three streets across, and if he had to guess, there were no more than a hundred people living here, at most.

On the far side of the main street stood another gate, past which he could see a winding path that led up to the temple, which sort of loomed over the entire town.

"Now, do we want to head straight up to the temple or go find a warm inn in which to get a hot meal and spend the night?" Keith asked, slowly walking down the street.

"I vote for the second option," Bob said, raising a small paw.

"Second option it is," Keith said, more than happy not to have to deal with any other pompous people for the rest of the day.

The chances of Gavin actually coming after him were extremely low. After all, if Keith were the gate guard, he wouldn't exactly want to report that he had let someone slip past after failing to so much as touch them. He would keep an eye on said person and plot his revenge for when they left the city. And Keith wasn't exactly worried about anything that Gavin would come up with.

It didn't take him long to find the town's only inn – a slightly shabby-looking structure with a faded sign out front – and head inside.

A small bell tinkled, getting the attention of the man snoozing behind the counter and startling him awake. The bottom floor of the inn wasn't much to look at. A small section containing a few tables was the only other thing on this floor. A set of stairs sat behind the counter, where Keith guessed the rooms were located.

"A new face," the innkeeper said, leaning forward and rubbing the sleep from his eyes. "I wonder what all the fuss is about lately, with all you newcomers showing up."

"I take it you've had a few visitors lately?" Keith asked.

"Eh, only a couple," the man shrugged. "Around here, though, that's quite uncommon. I do have to say that you look a lot less shady than the last bunch, muttering between themselves and wearing those long robes. Gave me the shivers. But they paid upfront and didn't damage the property, so I didn't ask any questions. Anyway, what'll it be?"

"A room for the night and a meal, if you've got one," Keith said.

"Sure thing," replied the old man. "That'll be fifty bronze for the room. Supper and breakfast will be included in that price."

Keith quickly did the math and found that it was still a bit pricey. Bob had told him the average room cost twenty-five bronze, and a meal was only seven. Still, since this was the only inn in town, the man could have tried overcharging him by a lot more. While Keith wasn't exactly happy to hand the money over, he did so without feeling resentful.

"Dinner will be served in half an hour," the man said, taking the money and handing him a key with the room number on it. "Breakfast is served from dawn to seven, and if you miss it, don't expect your money back."

"Got it," Keith said, taking the key and heading up the stairs.

There were only two doors, which made finding his room quite easy. Upon entering, he discovered that the room was exactly as he'd expected it to be. It had an old bed, creaky floorboards, and furniture that seemed to be on its last legs. There was a small heater in the corner, glowing a cherry red, and the walls kept the wind at bay. In short, it was warm, which was all Keith had really wanted.

"How much worse is the weather going to get?" he asked, stretching his arms overhead.

"Much worse," Bob replied. "You haven't seen anything yet."

Keith raised an eyebrow.

"Why do you think you got that cloak so cheap?" Bob probed, pointing to the article in question. "If you really think about it, a cloak that eliminates cold debuffs *and* keeps you pretty well insulated should have been much more expensive."

"I wouldn't say it keeps me well-insulated," Keith began, only for Bob to wave him off.

"You could be much colder, and you know it. The point is that cloaks like this are *very* common in the northern region of the continent, which is why it was so cheap. Trust me when I say that once winter really sets in, you won't be complaining about that cloak."

"I wasn't complaining," Keith protested.

"Sure you weren't," Bob said.

Seeing that he was getting nowhere with this and that it was a pointless argument, Keith decided to change the subject.

"What can you tell me about this Heavenly Temple Guild?" he asked.

"Well, as you've already noticed, they worship Naya, the Spirit of Light," Bob said. "They're one of the smaller guilds on the continent, as the main spirit worshiped here is Borg, Spirit of Sand. It's also the one worshiped by the Royal Guild."

"What about our guild?" Keith asked.

"The only thing they worship is a good weapon or mug of beer," said Bob, rolling his eyes. "But that's beside the point. The guild you need to learn from is very prideful, and the fact that you basically used a dirty trick to get into the city won't go over well with them."

"So what you're telling me is that this quest is impossible."

"No, it's still a B-difficulty quest, which likely means you'll need to pass some sort of test to qualify for a class."

"What classes will they have to offer? I saw that that man had an Iron Monk class, and to be honest, it didn't look all that impressive."

"No class looks all that impressive right out of the gate," Bob replied. "As for the classes they have available, I have no idea. Each temple will have different trainers, so I'm afraid you're on your own there."

Keith asked a few more questions, such as what it would take to get past the guard blocking the path up to the temple – to which Bob didn't know the answer – as well as several others.

He soon discovered the monkey's limit in what he knew. It seemed that while Bob knew a lot, certain specifics were beyond him. Keith likely would have remained there, asking questions, if not for the knowledge that they would be serving dinner soon. After having not eaten much that day, he was hungry.

Keith was disappointed with the plain meal of lukewarm broth and stale bread. He was almost tempted to ask for his money back, but in the end, he just decided to leave it in favor of going to sleep.

Now feeling irritable, Keith locked himself in his room and curled up on the lumpy bed, trying to ignore the gurgling in his stomach. He would have reached for his rations, but he needed them for his trip back to Oster's Keep and couldn't afford to dig into them to satisfy his hunger.

He was worried that he wouldn't be able to sleep that night, but much to his surprise, Keith felt himself drifting off quite easily. It seemed that the long day of travel in the freezing cold had sapped his energy to the point of exhaustion. Inside the warm room, out of the wind, he was soon fast asleep.

Keith's mind slowly pulled him back to the waking world. He blinked several times as his sleep-addled mind tried to figure out what had woken him. Having had his sleep interrupted many times over the course of his lifetimes, Keith knew what it felt like to be woken in the middle of the night.

Having dealt with many dangerous situations, he was also a light sleeper, and if his mind believed it was important for him to be up, it would wake him without mercy or hesitation, even if it was a false alarm.

Bob lay next to him, out cold on his back, his little stomach rising and falling in a steady rhythm. For several moments, Keith wondered what could have woken him. Then, he heard it. The barely audible sound of a voice talking on the other side of the wall.

It seemed the other guests the innkeeper had spoken of were awake. Keith was about to go back to sleep when a single sentence heard through the incoherent mumbling reached him.

"…that guild of monster hunters will get in the way…"

Instantly alert, Keith quickly moved from bed, careful to make as little noise as possible. Seeing as he was now part of the guild, any conspiracy involving them would also affect him. Besides, what were the odds that he would run into someone plotting something against his guild here of all places?

Moving stealthily to the far side of the room, Keith pressed his ear up against the wall and listened, the voices sounding far more clearly through the thin boards separating them.

"We have a plan for that," said a second voice, this one belonging to a woman. "All you need to do is make sure the correct items are in place, then we can...What was that?"

Keith had heard it as well. The telltale creak of floorboards in the hallway outside. It seemed that someone else was up there.

He remained where he was, listening carefully as the creak sounded again, followed by the sound of a key sliding into a lock.

"Someone's trying to sneak in," the woman said in a lowered voice that was barely audible. "Why don't you invite them in?"

Keith heard the sound of footsteps, followed by a surprised shout as the door was yanked open.

"Would you look who decided to come for a late-night visit?" the woman said, sounding a bit annoyed. "Did you think to use your spare key to sneak in here and try robbing us while we slept?" asked the woman as the sound of the door closing echoed through the wall.

"I...I wasn't planning *anything*. Honest."

The voice of the innkeeper, sounding slightly panicked, sounded next. It seemed the innkeeper had been planning on liberating him of his items. If his guess were correct, he would then have killed Keith and gotten rid of his body. It was unlucky for the innkeeper that these two happened to be awake when he'd tried entering their room.

"Do you know what we do to rats where I come from?" asked the male voice.

"I didn't do nothing! Honest," repeated the innkeeper.

"Well, it doesn't matter if you're innocent or not," the woman said. "You definitely overheard our conversation, which means we can't let you leave."

Keith heard a sudden commotion, followed by a loud crash, the wall he was pressed up against shaking a bit. A low groan sounded, much closer this time, as the innkeeper let out a whimper.

"Please," he croaked. "You don't have to kill me! I can help you."

"I very much doubt that," the woman said, sounding closer as well.

"I can! You're planning something with that monster-hunting guild in Oster's Keep, right? There's someone from the guild sleeping right next door."

Oh, that scumbag! Keith silently cursed the innkeeper, already moving away from the wall.

"Hey, wake up," he hissed, grabbing Bob around the waist and making for the door.

"What's goin' on?" the monkey asked, sounding half-asleep.

"We're in danger, so keep quiet until I say you can speak."

"Thanks for the information, old man," Keith heard through the door as he snuck into the hallway. "You were very helpful."

"I was?" the man asked, sounding hopeful. "Does that mean you're going to let me go?"

"Obviously not," the woman replied.

There was a loud cry that cut off halfway, turning into a wet-sounding gurgle as the innkeeper died. Keith was already at the stairs, ducking beneath the floor as the woman issued her orders.

"Go take care of the Pest Control next door. See if he's got any information we might find useful. We can't let anything interfere with our plans. Not when we're this close."

Keith wanted to wait to hear more but knew that he couldn't afford to stick around. The second they opened his door, they would see he wasn't there. Logically, they would assume he'd overheard them and set out after him.

He didn't know what chance he had of beating them both, especially since he had no idea how strong they were. Keith knew it was better to be safe and report back to the guild rather than trying to take them on by himself.

There was a loud crash as he ducked out of the inn and into the predawn air. It was freezing, and the cold immediately broke Bob out of his sleep.

"What's happening? Why are we out in the cold?" Bob complained just before Keith clamped a hand over his mouth.

"Keep it down," he hissed, ducking down behind the building and pulling the cloak tightly around him, hoping to be camouflaged by the poor light. "There are killers after us!"

Bob immediately stopped struggling and ducked beneath the cloak. Sure enough, a pair of cloaked figures burst from the inn just